Dear Reader,

Welcome to my world, where I work and play. California offers so much, enough to suit the most diverse tastes. Whether you're looking for surfing waves, giant redwoods, bountiful fruit and produce farms, deserts or the most sophisticated cities, we have them right here on the West Coast.

I've spent most of my life here. In my line of work I've done a fair amount of traveling. I enjoy seeing different parts of the world, but there's just something about coming home that makes me realize, over and over, that California is a very special place.

This book will tell you a little about me, about my life and about the only woman I've ever loved. I'll admit that we went through some really tough times, but love is worth fighting for. California was settled by people who were ready to fight to survive, so I guess some of that determination was passed down to me. It's a heritage to be proud of. Without it, I might not have the happiness I'm enjoying today.

Come and visit . . . anytime.

Regards,

Drew Donovan

California

ANNETTE BROADRICK

Deceptions

California

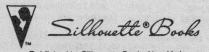

Silhouette Books

Published by Silhouette Books New York

America's Publisher of Contemporary Romance

SILHOUETTE BOOKS
300 East 42nd St., New York, N.Y. 10017

One

"**P**lease don't ask me, Adele," Lisa pleaded, her anguish apparent in her voice. "I couldn't bear to do it!" She jumped up from the comfortably padded chair in front of her agent's mammoth desk and agitatedly strode to the window.

"But, Lisa—" Adele Benton attempted to say.

"Surely you can understand that I can never make another movie with Drew Donovan!" She stared out the window at downtown Burbank, California, fighting to keep her composure.

"Lisa, listen to me. The role is perfect for you—it could have been written for you." She didn't want to admit the part *had* been written for Lisa. Not yet.

"*Sands of Sierra* will be filmed on location near Cuernavaca, Mexico. The hacienda is gorgeous. You'll be staying there as well as using the property for part of the filming. It will make a relaxing change from that hectic schedule you've been chasing."

"Fine. Then let them get another leading man. Anyone but Drew." Lisa continued to stare out the window.

Adele rose gracefully from her chair and quietly approached Lisa. "The producer wants both of you, Lisa. That's what I've been trying to tell you. These period movies are chancy at best, and they need bankable stars to ensure the public will at least turn out—even if it's only to see the two of you on screen together again." She waited for the diminutive actress to absorb the information she was hearing. Lisa's black, almond-shaped eyes stared at her, the pain within them causing Adele to suffer a twinge of guilt until she recalled what she was trying to accomplish.

"There is no way I can work with Drew again. Please don't ask that of me."

Adele studied her for a moment in silence. Lisa's midnight black hair tumbled around her face and over her shoulders, almost touching her waist. The woman was beautiful—and fiery—and a damned good actress. But she was also sensitive and extremely vulnerable, particularly where Drew Donovan was concerned.

Adele recognized that Lisa was that rare and intriguing person practically extinct in Tinsel Town—she was real, with no pretensions and no desire to be cloaked with the aura of a star. She was a professional in her field—dedicated, nontemperamental, a worker. She accepted her sultry good looks as a tool to be used in her career but never as a means to manipulate. It was no wonder to Adele that everyone with whom Lisa came into contact loved her. Drew Donovan most of all.

"Lisa," Adele said softly, "all I'm asking is that you consider co-starring with Drew in another picture. I'm not asking you to reconcile your marriage."

Lisa spun away from the window, her movements as rapid as a hummingbird's, and started pacing.

"I thought you understood what I've been going through, Adele. I really did." Her hair rippled around her shoulders as she turned away. "I'm finally functioning again—on a limited basis, maybe—but I'm managing all right." Her eyes pleaded for understanding. "But I'm not ready to see him again, Adele. I'm not even sure I'll ever be able to be comfortable around him."

Adele had never understood the reason for the breakup. All she knew was that shortly after their baby had been stillborn, Lisa had left Drew. A few months later she'd filed for divorce. That had been six months ago. She had refused to discuss her actions with Adele, either then or now, and Adele no longer expected to find out her reasons. But she could see that Lisa was still suffering, and she knew Drew wasn't doing any better.

Adele had decided that something had to be done for those two people. They had been a perfect couple, loving, sharing a strong love for acting, supportive of each other and loyal to their commitment to each other—all very rare qualities in any profession, but practically unheard of in the acting profession.

Once again Adele followed her client, this time taking her hand and patting it. "Sooner or later you're going to have to quit running, Lisa, and face yourself and Drew. Why not now?"

Lisa's eyes filled with treacherous tears. Adele was right. Sooner or later she would have to face him. But not now. Please, dear God, not just yet. During the past twelve months she'd spent her time everywhere but the West Coast. She'd done a film in Greece, then spent several weeks traveling in Europe—trying to come to terms with her own feelings and how she intended to survive the rest of her life, because Lisa Renee was a survivor. She'd worked hard perfecting her craft, spending years with lessons from the most famous of teachers. After her first major role, in a movie ironically named *Destiny*, Lisa had never looked back.

She'd been a star when she met Drew Donovan. So had he. They had met on location while filming *Red Sunset* five years ago.

Red Sunset had been a roaring success. And why not? The sensual current running between the two stars had been carefully documented by the all-seeing eye of the camera. Lisa had viewed the rushes and blushed. It was a wonder the celluloid hadn't melted during the love scenes!

Adele interrupted her thoughts. "The producer seems to feel that the public wants more romance these days. He wants to please them as well as make a few bucks. What's wrong with that?"

"But a historical?"

"It's time for a new trend, my dear. We need some swashbuckling heroes and dashing heroines to applaud—and villains to hiss. This script has it all." Adele unobtrusively watched Lisa's reactions. In this business, timing was everything. Adele hadn't gotten where she was today without knowing that.

Twenty-five years in the business had taught her a lot. She'd helped make stars, Lisa included. But Lisa was special to her—the daughter she'd never had or was ever likely to have, because Adele was successfully married to her agency.

She wanted to see Lisa happy again. In her heart she knew this was the only way. Drew and Lisa had to see each other again, had to spend time together in order to work out their problems. The new script had been a godsend.

Lisa sank into her chair once more. Her decision to leave Drew and to allow him to get on with his life without her had been the most difficult decision Lisa had ever made. She had since discovered it was a decision equally difficult to live with. But she had no choice, not if she loved Drew. The one constant in her life, the one unchanging factor that she lived with, was the knowledge that she would always love Drew Donovan. She loved him enough to set him free.

She stared at the silver-haired woman across the desk from her. What would she have done without her sensible agent's sage advice over the years? Adele seemed to have a sixth sense about the movie world, and Lisa had cause to be grateful for her guidance. But at the moment, Adele didn't realize just how vulnerable Lisa was—particularly where Drew was concerned.

"I can't."

The two words floated around the room, expanding and contracting, telling of lost dreams and hopes and the fear of further pain.

Adele walked around her desk and sat down behind it once more. She adjusted the glasses on the end of her nose, patted her perfectly coiffed silver hair, then folded her hands on the desk blotter in front of her.

"I'm not supposed to tell you." She kept her eyes on her hands.

Lisa looked up from pleating and unpleating the silky material of her skirt. "Tell me what?"

"Morey swore me to secrecy when he told me."

Morey Arnett had been Drew Donovan's agent since he'd first moved to the West

Coast. It had been a profitable association for both of them.

Lisa gripped the armrests of her chair with graceful hands and carmine-tipped nails. She'd never heard that tone from Adele before and she knew it was bad, whatever it was. *He's dying!* Lisa thought. *Something's wrong with Drew and I'm not supposed to know.* Her heart suddenly gained twenty pounds and sank in her chest. With a tortured expression, she gazed at Adele's carefully composed face.

"Tell me."

Adele's keen blue eyes finally met Lisa's. "It's not my secret."

"Tell me, Adele! What's wrong with Drew?" In her agitation she leaped up from the chair once more.

With slightly lifted brows, Adele stared at her until Lisa meekly sat down. Drew had often pointed out that she was too intense, too volatile—that she needed to learn how to relax and enjoy life as it came. Lisa agonized—from the time she first read a part and wanted it, during the time Adele was keeping her posted on negotiations, right up until the time she signed the contract. Then she agonized over learning her part, getting into the role. In short, Lisa was a worrier.

Such as now. "He's sick, isn't he?"

"Who, Morey? No, I don't think so. We had lunch together on Tuesday, and I thought he looked fine. He's even lost a few pounds."

"Adele, you know very well I'm not talking about Morey. What's wrong with Drew?" She leaned forward in her chair.

"Hmm. Drew. Yes, Morey did say it was all very unfortunate."

"What is, Adele?" she pleaded. "You're driving me out of my mind. Please tell me. What's wrong with Drew?"

Adele fixed her steady gaze on Lisa. "I have never divulged a confidence in my life. You don't last long in this business that way."

Lisa leaned even farther toward Adele so that she was perched on the edge of her chair, in real danger of sliding off completely except for the tight grip she had on the armrests. "I would never repeat anything told me in confidence. You know that, Adele. You've known me for ten years."

Adele continued to study the anxious expression, the fear in the eyes. Yes. It was time.

"Drew needs this film, Lisa." Lisa stared at her blankly. "It seems that Drew made some heavy investments earlier in the year that didn't pan out and he needs a successful movie right now. As I explained earlier, each of you will make substantial salaries as well as a tidy percentage of the profits. He's hurting, honey. But the producer is adamant. The pair of you—or nothing."

Lisa continued to stare at her agent in shock. Drew needed money? Drew Donovan? The only thing he took seriously was his money. He'd taught her all she knew about finances and diversifying—cautioning her to remember the unpredictability of their chosen profession. He was the most financially conservative man ever to set foot on the gold-dust trail toward cinema glory.

"Drew's broke?" she finally managed to whisper.

Adele gave a tiny negative shake to her head. "Not broke, my dear, just hurting." She unfolded, then carefully refolded her hands. "You know, a good vehicle is hard to find out here. And when you find a good script it can be hard to find backing. *Sands of Sierra* is one of the best scripts I've read in months, and the money's there—for the team of Donovan and Renee." It was time to draw the curtain. Adele briskly rose from her chair.

"Think about it, Lisa, then give me a call in a day or two." It was clearly a dismissal. "You've made it clear to the world that you no longer care anything about Drew. Well, now you have the chance to ruin him if you wish. He's at your mercy."

Lisa didn't remember leaving Adele's office, but found herself standing on the sidewalk staring blankly at her car. What was she going to do? How could she possibly work with Drew again? The pain would be debilitating. Could she see him, be around him, treat him as just an acquaintance?

Impossible.

Luckily traffic wasn't so heavy that Lisa had to be attentive on her way home, because she was distracted by memories of another time, another place. When she reached her condominium, Lisa wandered through the empty rooms, remembering five years ago, when she'd first met Drew....

Lake Tahoe was as beautiful as Lisa had always heard. She felt very fortunate to be filming on location there. *Red Sunset* was a Western, her first, and she was co-starring with Drew Donovan, also a first for her.

She stared out over the vista spread below the restaurant terrace of the hotel where the cast and crew were staying. The scenic mountains surrounding the emerald lake touched a responsive chord somewhere deep inside her, and Lisa basked in the quiet tranquility of the scene.

"Beautiful place to make a movie, isn't it?"

The sudden voice speaking directly behind her caused Lisa to jump, and strong hands clasped her shoulders to steady her. She spun around and faced the man who'd spoken.

Of course Lisa recognized Drew Donovan. Most females old enough to watch a movie screen would. He was a perfect specimen of virile manhood—tall, broadshouldered, muscular, with hips and thighs that looked great in whatever he wore, whether he was dressed for a Western or in another period costume. With his firm jawline and well-defined brows, his face was too strong to be labeled handsome. Drew's mouth saved him from looking austere—a humorous tilt usually lurked around its corners. The friendliness gave an openness to his appearance that everyone found appealing.

Although she'd been in the business long enough to become established, Lisa was still nervous about making this film with Drew. She'd never met him and had been experiencing definite qualms. Her fears were definitely justified. How would she ever be able to concentrate on her lines around him? Up close he was devastating.

He tilted his head slightly while he watched her, a slow smile spreading across his face. "Did your mother warn you not to speak to strangers, Lisa Renee? Then let me introduce myself. I'm Drew Donovan, your co-star for the next several weeks."

The top of Lisa's head barely reached his shoulder. Standing so close to him, she was forced to arch her neck in order to look him in the eye.

"I'm pleased to meet you," she murmured, distracted when he took her hand and held it between both of his.

"Not half as pleased as I am. I refuse to admit the number and amount of bribes I've offered to have the chance to do a film with you."

Lisa blinked in surprise. "Are you serious?"

His sherry-colored eyes sparkled. "Oh, yes. I'm very serious. I've enjoyed your films very much."

"I feel the same way about yours."

"Great. Then our mutual admiration society is off to a good start." He glanced around at the cluster of tables on the terrace. "Have you eaten?"

"Not yet."

"Why don't we find a table and get acquainted?"

Bemused, Lisa allowed him to lead her to one of the tables.

"I want you to tell me everything about yourself. I've already ascertained the most important statistic—you aren't married." Drew picked up the glass a waiter had just filled with water and toasted her. "The most obvious question is why not?"

Is this really happening? Lisa wondered. Drew Donovan sat across from her, his arms leaning on the table, studying her intently. It had never occurred to her that he would even know of her existence. Why should he be so interested? It was a well-known fact that he had never married, but she would never be so bold as to ask why. Obviously he preferred a single existence.

"I've never really tried to explain my reasons," she finally said. "I love my work, but it is exacting. I've been spending all my energy building a career. If and when I ever marry, it will be more than a matter of convenience. I want a strong, supportive marriage, like my parents have." She wished he wouldn't stare at her quite so intently. It was only her stage training that stopped her from fidgeting under his scrutiny.

"Tell me about your parents. Do you come from a large family?"

Lisa smiled. "Three older brothers and a sister two years younger than me. My folks have a large farm in Missouri. My brothers are all married and have big families. My sister is an attorney in St. Louis."

"How did it feel to grow up in a large family?" Drew asked wistfully.

"I take it you didn't have one, or you'd never ask."

"No. I have no family." He glanced up at the waiter, who was ready to take their order. After giving him their selections, Drew deftly changed the subject. "How long have you lived in California?"

"I moved out here six years ago."

"You must have been a baby."

"Not quite," Lisa admitted dryly. "I was twenty."

"That's still quite young. You seem so untouched by all the hoopla that surrounds the industry. That's one of the reasons I wanted to meet you, to get to know you better."

"*One* of the reasons? You mean there are more?"

"Certainly. But I never give away all my secrets at the first encounter." He leaned back in his chair and studied her. "When can I see you again?" he asked abruptly.

Lisa felt herself growing warm. "We start shooting tomorrow."

He nodded. "I know. So how about having breakfast with me...and lunch... dinner..."

"Drew!" Lisa started laughing. He was really outrageous.

He leaned toward her, his face solemn. "I'm serious, Lisa. I want to get to know you. I want you to get to know me. It's important."

Lisa gazed into the warm depths of his eyes and saw the sincerity there. If this was one of his lines, it was certainly effective. Actually, it was positively lethal to her peace of mind.

Lisa felt as though she was stepping on a carnival ride when she answered. "When do you want to meet for breakfast?"

By the time the location shots for *Red Sunset* were completed, Lisa felt that Drew had always been a part of her life. They had most of their meals together. Drew took her hiking; they went swimming, rented horses and went exploring through the mountains. At times Drew treated her as though he were her older brother. He seemed to delight in teasing her and playing jokes. His humor was contagious, and Lisa often found herself convulsed at some of his antics.

At other times he was the romantic figure that had always stood on the periphery of her imagination, waiting for his cue. Although he was an affectionate person, one who enjoyed touching, he made few overtures off the set other than a gentle goodnight kiss at the door to her hotel room, which was just as well. The script had a few torrid love scenes that more than made up for what wasn't happening in their private lives.

His on-screen lovemaking melted Lisa into a bubbling caldron of sensuous yearning. She longed to learn more about the passionate side of her nature. Yet he never took advantage of their situation. Never before had Lisa been as affected by anyone as she was by Drew.

During their last day on location, Drew walked over and casually draped his arm around Lisa's shoulders. "How are you going back to L.A.?"

Lisa glanced up in surprise. "Flying. Isn't everyone?"

"I thought I'd rent a car and drive back. There's a place I wanted to visit on the way. Would you like to ride along with me?" Although his tone was casual, his expression was intent, as though her answer meant a great deal to him.

And what could she answer? She'd like to go anywhere with him, but was that the best thing for her? Their time together had been something out of a dream, a fantasy of sorts, but it was time to return to reality.

"I'm not sure, Drew...."

"Do you have to be home at any particular time?"

"Not really."

"Then come with me. We should get back to L.A. by Friday—Saturday at the latest."

Which means we'll be spending the nights somewhere together. Not a very wise move if you don't want to get too involved, Lisa reminded herself.

"I'm not trying to coax you into anything but sharing the ride with me, Lisa. You will be as safe with me as you want to be."

What a provocative statement. He was placing the responsibility for what happened next squarely on her. She studied him for a moment. "All right, Drew. When do you want to leave?"

Two days later they were following the scenic coast south of San Francisco. Lisa had discovered she had nothing to fear but her own reactions to Drew. The first night they had stayed in a Sacramento hotel, in separate rooms. The next night they stayed in San Francisco, after exploring the sights around the city. Again, in separate rooms.

Lisa couldn't remember ever being so relaxed with anyone before. Drew made a marvelous companion. She had laughed at how well he could camouflage himself so that few people recognized him. One lady had commented that he looked very much like Drew Donovan, the movie star, and he'd gravely thanked her for suggesting there was a resemblance.

Lisa was used to not being recognized. The audience didn't realize how small she was, how easily overlooked in a crowd, and in her jeans and casual tops, she blended in with her surroundings. The sultry cinema beauty was nowhere in evidence.

Drew turned off the highway and began to follow a winding road that led into the hills overlooking the Pacific Ocean.

"Where are we going?"

"I have some friends up here I wanted to see."

"Oh, Drew. You should have said something. I'm not dressed for meeting anyone!"

He glanced over at her with a smile. "You look fine. They're going to love you."

"Who are they?"

"The closest family I have. They don't see me as a movie star. They accept me as one of them."

At the time, his comment meant nothing to Lisa, and she eagerly looked forward to meeting the people who caused such an eagerness in Drew. They must be very special.

A large fence appeared alongside the road, and when they came to a driveway, Drew stopped the car and got out, opened a large wrought-iron gate, drove through, stopped and closed the gate, then continued up a driveway.

A long, rambling Spanish-style adobe house sat on the crest of a hill, looking as though it had been built during the previous century—or even before. Large trees surrounded the home, casting welcome shade for the travelers.

Drew had no sooner stopped the car than the front door burst open. A sudden cacophony split the tranquil silence as several children ran down the steps and surrounded the car.

"It's Drew! Drew's here!"

"Go tell Miz Stratton. Drew's here!"

"Hi, Drew. How ya been?"

Drew stepped out of the car and was immediately surrounded by several laughing children of all ages. Lisa could see no resemblance among any of them. The only thing they had in common was the wide smile of welcome for Drew. Their ages ranged from about four to twelve or thirteen.

"Say, Tiger, won any ball games lately?" Drew asked the tallest boy there. The boy grinned bashfully.

"We've won the last three. Those pitches you showed me really helped."

Drew ruffled the curls on the boy's forehead. "Glad to hear it."

A tiny little girl was trying to shinny up Drew's leg. "Hold me, Drew. Hold me," she demanded imperiously.

Lisa watched him lift the young child high in the air, listened to her gurgle of laughter and felt a surge of emotion in her chest when he brought the girl to his chest and hugged her. "How's my favorite girl doing, Teresa?

Have you been a good girl for Ms. Stratton?"

She tucked her head down into his neck and nodded vigorously.

Drew turned around and saw Lisa still sitting in the car. He walked around to her side, Teresa still clinging to his neck. "I'm sorry, Lisa. I didn't mean to ignore you."

Lisa crawled out of the car and smiled at the boisterous children surrounding them. "You seemed to be busy."

He laughed, a young, relaxed sound that Lisa had never heard from him before. He draped his free arm around Lisa and headed toward the front door.

"C'mon. I want you to meet Beth Stratton."

Lisa would never forget that day. It was the day she'd acknowledged to herself that she was in love with the man the world knew as Drew Donovan. But he was so much more than his image suggested. She watched him work with the children, listen to them, talk with them, advise and console. He treated each child as though he or she was special to him, and it was obvious to Lisa that they were.

Beth Stratton had been charming. The middle-aged woman had the energy of ten people, it seemed to Lisa, and the patience and wisdom that bespoke a lifetime of loving and caring for others. She was a truly beautiful person, inside and out.

They were invited to spend the night, but Drew insisted they needed to be on their way. Lisa saw tears in the eyes of more than one child and was touched by the obvious affection all of them shared for Drew.

He was quiet for several miles after they were once again on the road heading south. "I'm glad you came with me today, Lisa."

"So am I. I really enjoyed meeting everyone."

"They enjoyed meeting you, too. I had to take a lot of teasing about having you along. I've never brought anyone before."

"You didn't want anyone to see the soft side of you?"

"No, that's not it. I've never wanted to share that part of my life with anyone before."

Lisa looked at him, his profile silhouetted in the late afternoon light. "I think what you're doing for those children is wonderful, Drew. You're adding something special to their lives. Are they orphans?"

"Yes."

"How did you find out about the place?"

"Simple. I was left on the front door when I was around two, or so the authorities guessed, and spent the next sixteen years of my life there." He glanced at her, then back at the road. "If I have parents, I've never known them. And I made a vow that when I left, I would never forget what it was like to live in a home without parents, without identity. I was determined not to let those who made their home there live without knowing they were loved."

Lisa heard the slight roughness in his voice, revealing some of the emotion he felt. To look at him, a person would think that Drew Donovan had the world in the palm of his hand. He had looks, intelligence, talent, and with those assets he had been able to acquire a great deal of money. Whoever the people were who had chosen not to raise the small child he'd been, they would never know how much they had missed. Any love they would have given him would have been returned tenfold.

She yearned to hold and love the tiny boy deep inside of him that still felt abandoned, but she didn't know how. She could only love the man who was beginning to reveal himself to her.

Perhaps that would be enough.

Two

For the next few months, Drew and Lisa spent as much time together as they could manage with their busy schedules. They both fought hard to be sensible about the fierce attraction that had sprung up between them. They had seen it happen too many times— falling in love with a co-star only to find that once the film was finished, so was the strong attraction.

Lisa was aware that Drew chose places for them to be together where they wouldn't be tempted to become intimate. He finally admitted to Lisa that once he made love to her, he would never be able to let her go.

During their time together, Lisa never brought up Drew's childhood, although she often wondered what scars it had left.

One day while they walked along the beach, she timidly broached the subject.

"Why were you never adopted, Drew?"

He was quiet for so long she decided he either didn't hear her or chose not to respond to her question. She wondered where she'd gotten the nerve to ask.

"Because no one knew anything about me," he finally answered. "Prospective parents want to know such things as family health problems . . . that sort of thing. Besides, I wasn't the most lovable little kid, you know." He smiled down at her, the sunlight making his eyes glitter.

"I can't believe that."

"They tell me I was scared of the dark and screamed whenever I was left alone . . . which in an orphanage doesn't happen all that often." He took Lisa's hand and slid his fingers between hers.

"Did they ever try to trace your parents?"

"No one knew where to start. They found me sitting in the driveway early one morning, crying. The tire tracks weren't traceable. At least I was abandoned at a place where I could receive care."

"Was there any note...or clothes?"

"Nothing."

"Oh, Drew."

"You know, Lisa, it sounds worse than it was. I mean, my earliest memories are of being treated kindly. I don't think I was ever abused. Someone just wasn't able to accept the responsibility of caring for me." He bent over and picked up a seashell, studied it for a moment, then stuck it in his shirt pocket. "I'll admit I spent years hoping to find a family that I could call my own—a home, people who loved me. I think that's when I first started fantasizing. I know that's why I've enjoyed acting so much. For a little while I can be anyone I want. I don't have to wonder who I am, what sort of people I came from."

"You give so much of yourself in your acting. There's a vulnerability that is generally missing with so many other actors. I've often marveled at the sensitivity you show."

"Thank you, fair lady. I could say the same about you."

Lisa chuckled. "Here we go again. Seriously, I wondered why you haven't married before now—you have so much to give to a relationship."

"Except a name."

"Is that really so important?"

"To some people."

Not to me, love, Lisa thought. *Not to me.*

In all their time together, Drew had never mentioned the future or where their relationship might be heading, and Lisa couldn't help but wonder about his feelings. He made it clear he was seeing no one else, but he made no sign that he wanted their friendship to deepen into anything more than the companionship they'd found.

Maybe he sees me as his long-lost sister. What a revolting thought. I'm supposed to be such a sex symbol. No one would believe the platonic relationship we have.

Lisa kept remembering how comfortable Drew was around the children. He was so obviously cut out to be a family man. Finally one afternoon she found the courage to bring up the subject.

"Do you want a family, Drew?" she asked while stretched out beside him on a lounge chair on the deck of his home.

He rolled over and leaned up on his elbow to peer down into her face. "Are you volunteering?" he asked with interest.

"Volunteering for what?"

"To help me start a family. I've often wondered how women approach seduction. I should have known you'd go in for the more direct approach."

Lisa sat up suddenly, nudging his elbow so that he lost his prop. "Dream on, cowboy. That was not the reason I asked."

He started laughing at the look of outrage on her face. "I can always hope, can't I?" He stretched out once more on the lounge. "Years ago I used to dream of being part of a large family. But like most of my dreams, that one was packed away with the rest of my childhood fantasies.

"I think I must have been about five years old when I discovered that those of us who lived at the San Luis home were different from other children. We had regular visitors, townspeople who cared and who brought us toys and books and periodically took a group of us out for the day. I realized that other children had a mother and father, or at least one of them to call their own."

He glanced at Lisa. "They tell me that for the first few months after I arrived I cried for 'Mommy,' so at one time she was very real to me. But I don't remember any of that."

Drew stared out at the waves, but he saw only memories. "I must have been about ten when Beth Stratton came to San Luis. Secretly I pretended she was my real mother and that she had come back in disguise to be sure I was all right." He smiled slightly. "She was and is a very understanding person. She gave so much of herself to each of us, making us feel very special. She gave me the closest example of motherhood I ever had.

"I grew up determined that someday I would establish a family of my own, but not before I had the time to devote to making them feel they had a father who loved them. I want to be with them on a daily basis, enjoy each new learning skill they develop, give them the security of knowing I will always be there.''

He touched her cheek. ''How about you? Do you want a family?''

Lisa smiled. If she were honest she would tell him that it had only been since meeting him that her daydreams of having a family had taken on a sense of yearning. ''Yes.''

Slowly Drew sat up. He leaned over and tugged Lisa to a sitting position. ''Since meeting you, I keep picturing myself surrounded by little black-haired boys and girls calling me Daddy. I can think of nothing that would give me more pleasure.''

He leaned over and kissed her, a soft, tentative kiss that caused shivers to tingle through her. Then he stood up and drew her to her feet, enclosing her in a loose embrace.

''Lisa, I don't know how you feel about us, but I love you so much that I feel like I'm going to explode with it. I want to love you, and live with you, and have babies with you. Lisa, love, please marry me."

Now that he was saying what she most wanted to hear, Lisa didn't know what to say. She felt a panicky tremor. To her, marriage was a permanent commitment, one not lightly entered into. A Hollywood marriage was even more fraught with peril. But if they both loved each other, wasn't that enough?

"Isn't it too soon?"

"For what? For me to love you? I have no control over that."

"We agreed to use this time to get better acquainted."

"We are. I have. And I already know enough about you to know I want to spend the rest of my life with you." He sounded very sure of himself. Very certain of his feelings. And Lisa wanted to believe him.

She studied his clear, tawny eyes and saw the love in them. It would work out. With the love they both felt for each other, they would be able to solve anything.

Sliding her hands up around his neck, she moved closer to him. "I love you, Drew

Donovan, more than I believed it possible to love anyone.''

''Then you'll marry me,'' he stated in an aggressive tone.

''Yes, I'll marry you,'' she agreed softly, pressing closer to him.

He scooped her up in his arms and walked into the house. Both of them had waited for this day, both had subconsciously known when Drew had suggested, and Lisa had agreed, to spend the day at his place that a decision would be reached for them.

Lisa clung to his broad shoulders while he strode down the hallway. She had never been in that part of the house. Now that the time had come, she was nervous, but she loved him too much to pretend she didn't want him to make love to her.

For a brief moment she wished she had more experience. At thirty, Drew was no innocent boy. He was a man with a man's needs and she could only hope that she would instinctively know how to fulfill those needs.

Drew seemed to sense her nervousness. He placed her gently on the mammoth bed, which dominated the spacious room. Lisa tried to remember all she'd learned from the parts she'd played. However, this was much different—no cameras, no director, and no script. All she had to go on was her desire to give pleasure to the man who was casually stepping out of his jogging pants at the side of the bed!

He was gorgeous. There was no other word to describe him. Suddenly, Lisa lost her self-consciousness. She wanted to touch him, to feel him close to her, to explore the smooth surface of his chest, following the beguiling trail of soft blond hair as it arrowed down from his navel.

"Lisa?"

"Hmm?"

"Aren't you going to get undressed?" Drew asked softly.

Oh. There she went, daydreaming, and she must have missed a cue. Lisa unsnapped her halter top, then unsnapped and unzipped the snug shorts she wore—not the most graceful way to get out of clothes, she was forced to admit.

Drew's hands fell on either side of her waist, and he began to slide her shorts down her legs. His lips followed the same path until her clothing lay forgotten on the floor. Then his mouth slowly moved back up again until it reached the satin of her bikini briefs.

"You're trembling," he whispered.

"Yes."

"Are you afraid of me?"

"Not exactly."

He paused in his loving exploration along the top edge of her bikini panties, his soft touch tickling the sensitive skin of her abdomen.

"Haven't you ever made love before?"

She shook her head.

He sat up suddenly. "Oh, Lisa, it never occurred to me to ask you before now."

She smiled. "I'm very glad I waited."

He pulled her close and whispered in her ear. "So am I, love, so am I."

Drew took his time kissing and caressing her. Slowly, Lisa felt the tension drain from her body. In its place came an emotional response to his touch that set her body to tingling. She felt dizzy with love for him. Never had anything seemed more right than to be there with Drew, and she showed him her pleasure by imitating his touch, his caresses, his sensual exploration, so that she became aware of her ability to affect him.

By the time he positioned himself over her, Lisa was eager for the next step. She could feel the fierce thudding of his heart and knew hers was keeping time with it. Her breath caught in her throat when she felt the full thrust of his passion. He paused. "I don't want to hurt you."

"You could never hurt me, Drew. I want you to show me how to express my love for you."

Slowly Drew began to move and she felt a tiny spark begin within her. She felt it glow, then spread throughout her body. Instinctively she responded to his movement, glorying in their closeness, recognizing the tenderness that he brought to their time of sharing.

Never had she loved Drew more than when she recognized his patience over the past few months. She knew they shared something very special, a precious gift that few couples ever experienced.

Then she could no longer think. Instead, Lisa became a creature of emotions and sensations that clung to Drew as she entered into a new dimension. He carried her to the farthest reaches of the universe, and she knew that nothing in her life would ever again be the same.

During the next three years they often talked about the family they wanted, and Drew expanded on how much a family would mean to him. Lisa had gone to a specialist to find out if there was a reason why she hadn't conceived, but the doctor found nothing to prevent a successful pregnancy.

She would never forget the day she got the wonderful news that their perseverance had paid off.

"Drew! We did it! We finally did it!" She ran into their beachside home exclaiming.

Drew sat out on the deck, enjoying the sun and fresh sea air, but he got to his feet in time to catch her when she threw herself into his arms. "That's marvelous, love! I knew we could." He gave her a long, intimate kiss, then asked, "What have we done?"

Lisa laughed. "Oh, this wasn't the way I was going to tell you. I had it all planned—you know . . . soft candlelight dinner, champagne, me in something sheer and flowing." She hugged him even closer. "Oh, Drew. I'm so happy."

He stared down into her shining face with a puzzled smile.

"We're going to have a baby," she murmured shyly.

"Well, how about that? We must have done something right during these past few months," he teased. Drew attempted a puzzled frown, but his dancing eyes gave him away. "Does this mean we can't continue to practice?"

"You're crazy, you know that?"

"Yes. I am absolutely, one hundred percent crazy over you. I don't believe it's curable."

"Oh, Drew. I love you, too. And now we're going to be able to have that family we've always talked about."

They had so much fun preparing the nursery. Drew enjoyed the shopping expeditions as much as Lisa, and Lisa learned a great deal more about the man she had married.

"What do you think?" he asked, holding up a mobile for her inspection. "Wouldn't this be nice to wake up to each morning?"

"Do you want to hang it over our bed?" Lisa asked.

"Not ours—the baby's."

"Oh."

"What if he or she wakes up early? We don't want the baby getting bored."

"Of course not. How sensible of you to point that out."

He pulled her into his arms. "Are you laughing at me?" he demanded.

"Never."

"Good." He glanced around. "How about some colorful curtains for the windows—you know, for stimulation."

"Anything you say, Drew."

Toward the end of the pregnancy Drew delighted in feeling the baby move. They were in bed and the lights were out. Lisa was having trouble getting comfortable, and Drew placed his hand on her protruding abdomen and began to gently stroke it. "Go to sleep, little one, go to sleep," he murmured. "Let your mommy get some rest."

The baby gave a vigorous kick.

"Do you think he has a basketball in there?" Drew asked.

"Right now it feels like the entire Harlem Globetrotters are in there." Lisa shifted, turning on her side.

"I wish I could help," Drew whispered, gently pushing her hair off of her forehead.

"You are, love. Having you here with me is all I need."

"Don't you get excited, thinking about having another person sharing our life together?"

"Yes. I think he's as anxious to get here as we are to have him arrive."

"Are you sorry we didn't find out the sex?"

"No. I wanted it to be a surprise. Whatever it is suits me."

"Me too. We can always have more."

"Um-hmm," Lisa sighed.

Drew began to massage her back, and Lisa drifted off to sleep, secure in the knowledge that he was there.

She would never forget the night she'd gone into labor. Drew had practised being calm for so long that he had almost been a zombie. Lisa would have believed he was taking the news that she needed to go to the hospital in stride if he hadn't started out the front door barefoot with her suitcase, wearing only a pair of cut-off jeans—in January.

They had laughed all the way to the hospital.

Her pains had been surprisingly easy, and it was only during the last stages of labor that problems developed. Drew was with her in the delivery room until the monitoring system on the baby's heart began to signal distress, then they'd sent him out.

The next few hours had been a nightmare. Drew stayed with her after they'd wheeled her back to her room. Everything had changed for them in a few short hours.

Drew sat beside her bed, holding Lisa's hand and stroking her face. "Nobody knows why these things happen, love, but we're going to make it through this time together, you and me. We love each other—that's what is important to remember. And we have each other.''

What would she have done without his support? He put his grief on hold and comforted her. And she needed that support so much.

Lisa felt inadequate, as though God were punishing her for some reason. Couldn't she be a good enough parent? Wasn't she even going to be given the chance to try?

When Lisa returned home she discovered that Drew had stored all the baby furniture and accessories they had purchased and had even taken down the colorful curtains so that there was no reminder in the bedroom of the baby that should have come home with her.

Lisa wrestled with her depression, determined not to let it pull her down or slow her recovery. She and Drew clung to each other during the following weeks and Lisa began to plan for another pregnancy as soon as the doctor said it was safe.

Then came her six weeks checkup and the nightmare became overwhelming.

"I'm afraid I have some bad news for you, Lisa," Dr. Jacobs told her.

Lisa sat across the desk from him, watching his kind eyes through his rimless glasses.

"All the tests we've run on you are fairly conclusive. We discovered that you carry in your genetic makeup a chromosome that under certain conditions will produce the problem that caused the death of your baby. There is no way to test this beforehand, but I would say the chances of you and Drew being able to have a baby survive birth is less than five percent." He slowly pulled off his glasses and began methodically polishing them with a handkerchief. "Not very good odds, I'm afraid."

Lisa sat there staring at him, waiting for the director to yell "Cut!" She waited for the scene to end and reality to surface. He couldn't be talking about her, not her and Drew. Not after all their plans, their dreams, their hopes for the future.

"Would you like me to call Mr. Donovan and explain the results of the tests to him?"

Since she hadn't even told Drew about the tests she had insisted on taking, she refused.

He would have told her she was worrying unnecessarily and to relax and accept whatever happened.

"I'll tell him, Dr. Jacobs."

Drew would understand. He loved her; he'd made a commitment to her; he would honor that commitment—no matter the cost to him. But could she ask that of him?

He had waited so long to marry. He wanted to be established in his career before starting a family. She knew how both goals had been so important to him. How many times had she sat and listened to all his plans during her pregnancy? He'd even planned when the second one should be conceived because he didn't want an only child! Now she had to tell him there would be no children. None at all.

Looking back, Lisa realized that she'd been in shock after her visit to the doctor. She could still remember calmly deciding to convince Drew she no longer wished to be married to him.

If she couldn't give him the family he wanted, then he needed to marry someone who could. She'd felt a keen determination to protect Drew from his own compassion-ate nature. If she told him the truth he would insist on their staying together.

She couldn't do that to him.

Lisa was deliberately late reaching home that evening. By the time she got out of the car Drew was at the front door and striding out to her.

"Lisa, are you all right? I've called ev-erywhere I could think of, trying to find you. Did you have car trouble? Why didn't you call me?" His arms came around her and he hugged her close. She felt the slight tremor of his hands on her back. She had fright-ened him, which hadn't been her intention.

What she had intended to do was to irri-tate him, provoke him, attempt to set up a situation where he would become angry.

Lisa had never felt so inadequate for a role in her life.

Forcing herself to step back from him, she coolly met the anxious look on his face. "I really don't need a keeper, Drew. I'm fine, just fine." She sidestepped him and walked into the house.

"Where have you been? Maria said you left right after lunch."

Drew followed her down the hallway to their bedroom. Lisa began to strip out of her clothing as though she were alone. Without looking at him, she asked, "Oh, is spying on me one of Maria's duties?"

"*Spying* on you! For God's sake, Lisa, what's wrong with you?"

She walked into the adjoining bathroom and turned on the shower. Piling her long hair on her head and securing it with pins, she said, "Nothing's the matter with me, Drew. What could possibly be wrong?"

The shower felt good, and she stood there wondering how she was going to get through that evening. She wasn't going to be able to stay with him even one more night. Because if she did, she knew she'd break down and tell him everything—her fears and confusion, her pain and frustration, her anger that her body could have betrayed her in such a fundamental fashion.

No. She had to get out tonight.

Drew was waiting for her in the bedroom when she came out of the bathroom. She stopped and looked at him without expression. "Were you waiting for something?"

He looked at her, confusion and a trace of pain etched on his face. "I thought maybe you'd be hungry. It's almost ten o'clock."

"I've already eaten," she lied calmly. Pulling out underwear from one of her drawers, she quickly dressed in slacks and a pullover knit top. She walked into the oversize closet she shared with Drew, picked up the empty suitcases stored there and brought them out.

Drew came to his feet, his color gone. "What in the hell do you think you're doing, Lisa?"

She forced herself to look him in the eye, forced herself to betray no expression and answered him. "I'm leaving you, Drew."

Drew stared at her as though she had pulled out a pistol and taken careful aim, then fired. Thinking back, Lisa realized that perhaps metaphorically that was what she had done. He slowly sank back down on the side of the bed. She barely heard his murmured, "Why?"

Lisa turned away, ostensibly to pack, but in reality because she could no longer bear to see what her words and actions were doing to him. She reminded herself why she was doing it and only from that could she draw the necessary strength to continue the charade.

"I would think that's obvious, Drew. I no longer want to be married to you." Hurriedly she threw her belongings in her suitcases, needing to escape before she broke down.

The silence in the room grew and expanded until it almost pushed the occupants out of the area with its intensity. Lisa felt Drew's pain as though it were her own, and in a way it was. She felt engulfed, almost suffocated by it.

"It's because we lost the baby, isn't it?" he finally asked quietly.

"It no longer matters why, Drew. Just accept the fact that I'm leaving." She refused to look at him. After glancing around to be sure she'd cleared the surface of her dresser, she carried her makeup bag into the bathroom and hurriedly began to fill it.

"You can't mean it." He stood in the doorway, watching her in disbelief, the pain and agony in him almost visible to her.

"Yes. This is something I have to do."

She turned around and waited for him to move. He continued to stare at her, then finally stepped back, allowing her to enter the bedroom once more.

"Lisa, honey, listen to me. Don't do this to us. We've got too much going for us, too much at stake to allow an impulsive decision to destroy what we've built together."

"This isn't an impulsive decision. I've been considering it for some time." Another lie, but a necessary one. Impulsive or not, this was one decision she had to stick to, and she couldn't afford to let him talk her out of it. He could very well do that if she stayed around him. He had powers of persuasion over her that were so strong that they should have been outlawed.

She picked up her two largest bags and started down the hall.

"Dammit, Lisa, I'm not going to let you do this!" He followed her down the hallway and yanked one of the bags out of her hand.

She turned around and slowly looked up at him, trying for a look of contempt by the time her eyes met his. "Do you intend to keep me here by force? Because that's the only way you can do it. I don't want to stay with you, Drew. Why don't you just accept that? I'd prefer not to have a scene, if you don't mind. I'm rather tired."

Drew looked at her as though her words were unintelligible, as though the language she spoke was beyond him. She could certainly understand that reaction. Then she leaned over and took the bag from him, turned around and walked to the front door, opened it, then carried her bag to her car, which she had purposely left outside the garage.

Returning to the house, she found Drew where she'd left him—standing in the hallway. She walked past, picked up her remaining bags and returned to the front door. "I'll check with Maria in a few days to be sure I didn't overlook something."

Lisa's stomach was beginning to churn, and she knew she only had a few moments to get out of there before her body betrayed her. She glanced over her shoulder. Drew had not moved from his position in the hallway. "I'll be in touch, Drew." When she closed the door behind her, she whispered, "Please be happy, love. For both our sakes, please be happy."

She was only a few blocks away from the house when she had to pull over. Lisa was too sick to drive, too sick to care what happened now. She had done it. She'd removed herself from Drew's life. . . .

That had been almost a year ago. During that year Lisa worked at making a new life for herself. She had finally forced herself to see an attorney and begin the legal proceedings that would finally sever the relationship. She only wished it were as easy to sever all the emotional ties she felt for him.

Lisa determinedly turned over in the bed and glanced at the small digital clock on her bedside table. It was almost four o'clock in the morning.

Adele had no idea what she was asking of Lisa. What was she going to do?

Three

─────

On the sixth floor of a prestigious bank building in downtown Los Angeles, Drew Donovan sat staring at Morey Arnett in disbelief.

"Are you out of your mind?" Drew asked incredulously, running his hand through already rumpled tawny hair. He glared at his agent, convinced that Morey had finally slipped over the edge and was only now waiting for commitment.

Morey laughed. A slender man of indeterminate age, Morey was seldom if ever at a loss for words, and he had a mind that generated ideas and plans with a speed reminiscent of a whirlwind. He had a great deal of power in the movie industry, which was common enough, and wielded it wisely, which was very uncommon.

"Come on, you know that your greatest films have been made with Lisa Renee." He leaned back in his chair. "Let's see, how many have there been?"

"Three," Drew bit off tersely.

Morey's hands came up behind his head, and he locked his fingers together. "Any how many Academy Awards were you nominated for?"

"Three," Drew responded more slowly.

"No doubt a coincidence. Although I have to admit that when someone as lovely as Lisa Renee gives you those melting looks from her gorgeous eyes, we all tend to think you're as special as she obviously does."

"She's an actress, dammit. She's paid to look at me that way."

"You each won the award, as I recall, different years." He smiled. "I always wondered if that was why the two of you split—two careers in the family and all. Tell me, Drew, was she too much competition for you?"

Drew leaped from his chair, then realized how well Morey knew him. He shook his head. "You really are a bastard, Morey. Why are you baiting me? If it were up to me, Lisa and I would still be together and you know it."

"So why don't you want to do *Sands of Sierra* with her?" Morey watched his client pace in front of him and marveled once again at nature's inequities. Why should one man have so much going for him? Not only was he extremely intelligent, but he also had the kind of character that no amount of fame or fortune could corrupt. Wouldn't that be enough for any one person? Not in Drew's case. He also looked like a million bucks. Although his face was too strong to be labeled handsome, from the amount of fan mail he'd received since his first minor role, it was obvious that women liked what they saw. Maybe that jawline denoted a little more stubbornness than was necessary, but the wide, often smiling mouth effectively compensated. Most of the time.

Today the mouth looked every bit as determined as the jawline. Morey sighed. He must be getting old. He didn't know why he was willing to put himself through this nonsense. But he knew why. Adele Benton.

He wasn't sure when Adele managed to wrap herself around his heart. It was a secret he intended to keep until he died. But when she asked him to help her pull this deal off, he'd found himself staring into those clear blue eyes and promising her anything.

He straightened in his chair. "Look, Drew, I don't care if you do this damned film or not. It's nothing to me. I sure as hell don't need the money. Neither do you. It's just a shame Lisa was stupid enough to get herself in a bind."

Drew stopped his pacing and spun around. "What do you mean?"

Morey had the grace to look ashamed. "Forget that. I wasn't supposed to say anything."

With two strides Drew was leaning on the desk, staring at Morey. "What's happened to Lisa?"

"What do you care? She's not your responsibility any longer, remember? She walked out on you—hurt you like hell. She deserves everything she's getting."

Drew spaced his words carefully through clenched teeth. "What's happened to Lisa?"

Morey shrugged. "I don't know, exactly. I had lunch with Adele the other day and she said Lisa had made some poor investments or something. I don't know. Must need the money pretty badly."

Drew stared at his agent for a moment. "You mean Lisa has already agreed to make this picture?"

"It doesn't do any good for only one of you to agree. The offer is both—or neither. I told Adele I'd mention it to you, but I've already warned her what your answer would be."

Drew slowly straightened, then turned away from Morey, walking over to the window and staring out without seeing anything.

Lisa. He hadn't been able to sleep for months after she'd left. She haunted him. Everywhere he turned in their home overlooking the Pacific he saw her, or heard her tinkling laugh, or faced her teasing smile. When he did sleep he dreamed of her. His brain replayed tapes of their life together.

He saw her glossy black curls spilling over the ivory satin pillow case, her petite body perfectly formed and seductively arrayed in a flesh-toned lace and satin excuse for sleeping apparel. She'd never managed to go to sleep in it.

Those magnificent eyes invited him closer, always closer, their slight tilt at the corners giving her an exotic look that mesmerized him. And she had been his—all his.

When they'd found out she was pregnant, their lives appeared complete, and when their tiny daughter had failed to live, he'd felt that part of him had died as well.

He'd tried to convince Lisa there could be others. The doctor had been vague about the cause of death. There had been some talk about congenital disorder, something that none of them had control over.

He'd waited for Lisa to come to terms with her grief, to accept their loss and go on. Instead, she had grown increasingly distant until the day she'd announced she was leaving him—she no longer wished to be married.

He had tried to convince her they could work things out together. That they loved each other enough to overcome all obstacles. But nothing he'd said seemed to affect her. He'd loved her as he'd never loved anyone before, but his love hadn't been enough.

And now she needed money. It was ridiculous, really. After Lisa left, she had refused to take any money from him. She wanted nothing from him—which had hurt him even more. Even her attorney had grown frustrated with her stubborn stand. But that was Lisa. Stubborn to a fault. Also full of courage and determination. And he still loved her. Dammit!

She wouldn't let him help her financially, but she was willing to make a movie with him. Maybe willing was too strong a word. From the sound of things, neither of them was being given too much choice.

But he didn't need the work, he reminded himself. He'd managed to survive losing her by drowning himself in a sea of scripts and scenes, moving from location to location without thought or concern. As long as he didn't need to go home to that empty, echoing house, which would always be empty— regardless of the number of people in it— because Lisa wasn't there.

Morey patiently waited for Drew to make the only decision possible for him, knowing how he felt about Lisa. He felt a slight twinge of conscience, but only a slight one. Not that he was at all sure Adele was right. But he was willing to go along with the plan.

Eventually Drew turned around and faced his agent and long-time friend. He looked tired. Even worse, he looked defeated. "When do we start filming?"

Adele's phone rang and she grabbed it.

"He just left." Morey's voice sounded so clear that he could have been in the next room.

"And?"

"He bought it."

Adele burst out laughing. "That's marvelous, Morey. I knew you could do it!"

"Not me, sugar, not me. You knew good and well that Drew would gallop to her rescue if he thought she needed him."

She smiled. "Let's just say that I hoped."

"How did your side go?"

Adele's smile expanded into an impish grin. "Actually, I think I missed my calling, Morey. I really should have been an actress. You would have been proud of me."

There was a moment of silence while Morey fought the impulse to say what he really felt—*I'm always proud of you.* Instead, he asked in a gruff tone. "The question is, is she going to do it?"

"Of course she is. She just hasn't faced it yet!"

"You're pretty damned sure of yourself."

"No, I'm sure that those two are still very much in love with each other and that they need this opportunity to spend some time together."

"And they'll probably end up like two icicles on the set. Remember, this is supposed to be a love story."

"I know," Adele said. "I sent the script home with Lisa, told her to read it and get back to me. There's no way she'd turn down the chance to help Drew in his time of need—" she chuckled "—and when she sees what a good part she has, she's bound to take it."

"Keep me posted. Remember, if we pull this off, you've promised me a weekend in Acapulco."

Adele fingered the phone cord a little nervously. "So I did. I must have had too much to drink to make such a rash promise."

"Don't worry, kid. You won't have to do any running to get away from me. Not at my age. My chasing days expired some time ago."

The amusement in his voice reminded Adele that Morey had made his reputation around town by squiring the most beautiful and talented women to the most widely publicized events. "I refuse to get into a debate over your virility at this point, Morey. As I recall, the offer was for you to take the companion of your choice."

"So it was. I'll keep that in mind."
"I'll call you as soon as I hear anything."
"You do that."

Lisa lay curled up in her king-sized bed, looking like a little girl in her nightshirt and pigtail. She dropped the script of *Sands of Sierra* on the bed beside her and stared into space.

It was a beautiful love story. She could see Drew playing the role of Reynaldo, the renegade who fell in love with Conchita, the daughter of the owner of the hacienda and surrounding countryside. A classic love story. With his tawny hair and eyes, he'd look magnificent in the black period costumes.

Drew. She'd fought for so long to erase him from her mind, but the moment she'd quit fighting, the memories had all tumbled back. She had spent the past three days trying to ignore the script Adele had given her, trying to find the courage to call Adele and tell her she would not do the film.

She hadn't been able to do it. Lisa wasn't sure whether reading the script had been an act of courage or cowardice. It had lain on her bedside table and beckoned to her. Drew needed to make the movie, and she was the only one who could help him.

With sudden decision, she sprang out of bed and strode to the television set. Digging under the cabinet she found the video of *Red Sunset*. She quickly placed it in the recorder and turned it on.

For the next two hours Lisa became lost in the movie and her memories of Drew. She could remember the feel of his arms around her, the taste of his lips possessing her, the joy of knowing he loved her. Forgotten was the pain of giving him up and learning to live without him.

Drew needed her. He needed to star in this new film and she could help him. Was she still so wrapped up in her own grief that she wouldn't even help the man she loved when he needed her?

It's time to crawl out of the hole you've been hiding in, Lisa, old girl. You made your decision—now live with it like an adult.

Drew must not be concerned about seeing her again or he wouldn't have agreed to make the movie. He must be reconciled to the divorce by now.

She really had no choice. Her feelings were *her* problem and she would have to deal with them.

She'd call Adele tomorrow and tell her she'd make the film.

Four

The Mexican countryside looked hot and dry, and Lisa was thankful the limousine that had met her at the Mexico City airport was air conditioned. Cuernavaca was some sixty miles south of Mexico City, and she'd found herself speculating on whether Drew would be at the Hacienda Vista Hermosa when she arrived.

She had asked no questions. Instead, she'd left all arrangments to Adele and had buried herself in the script, trying to become Conchita with her fear of her father and his absolute control over her life, and with her love for Reynaldo. How horrible it must have been back in those days not to have had any say in the direction of your life, to know that first your father, then your husband, had absolute control over your person and your possessions.

She couldn't imagine anything like that. Her marriage had been a partnership in which decisions had been arrived at after discussion, but never arbitrarily. She smiled, remembering some of those discussions that had become a little noisy. She knew she worried too much—about everything. Because of her insecurity she would automatically take the advocate role in a discussion to ensure that they didn't overlook a possibility or two.

Drew used to tear his hair when, after several hours of weighing the pros and cons, she would finally admit that she had agreed with him all along.

She had never fully appreciated the fact that he listened to her, weighed her opinions carefully and with respect. At the time she had taken his attitude for granted. But it had been one of his many lovable traits.

The limousine turned off the highway onto a narrow paved road that was soon bordered on one side by a white stucco wall. Lisa realized the wall was part of the hacienda when the car slowed down and turned between two wrought-iron gates.

For a moment Lisa thought she'd discovered a movie set already prepared for filming. A winding road ran ahead of them, lined on either side by blooming poinciana trees, their lush, fiery flowers adding a dreamlike appearance to the roadway. Although everything on the other side of the wall had been brown and dry, the grass and shrubs inside were luxuriantly green, the glossy leaves shining in the sunlight.

They passed through an archway of another wall around the hacienda itself and pulled into a circular driveway.

The limousine had barely stopped when Lisa's door was pulled open. "Lisa, my dear, it's delightful to see you!"

Tom Trevayne, the director of the movie, as well as a long-time friend, grasped her hand and helped her from the car. With his sandy hair and lightly freckled face, Tom looked younger than his forty-plus years. He and Lisa had worked together before and she was relieved to have him involved in this picture.

"It's good to see you too, Tom. Are you the one responsible for my reception at the airport?"

He grinned, his brown eyes dancing. "A little publicity never hurt a picture, Lisa. I had intended to meet you myself, but as usual I had a crisis to settle here." He gave her a quizzical look. "Was it very bad?"

"No. Not really. The chauffeur handed me your note, and he was very efficient with my luggage." She glanced around the place. "What a beautiful spot to be on location."

Tom looked around as though the surroundings were his own personal creation. "Isn't it, though?" They both enjoyed the view of the sparkling swimming pool with the stone arches running through the center of it so that it was actually two very large swimming areas. He put his arm around her shoulder and started up the steps. "At one time this was an honest-to-God working hacienda, but for the past several years it's been a resort. They maintained the ambience of the place, though. Just wait until you see some of the main rooms—the wide-planked floors, the old smoked beams, the painting of the senorita dressed in all her finery over the fireplace. Talk about atmosphere. The place is oozing with it." Lisa wondered why Tom appeared nervous. He kept glancing at her while he talked, his eyes concerned.

Of course. He's worried about how Drew and I will get along now that we're separated. Tom had directed them in two other pictures, and she could see why he might be wondering how they'd react to each other now. Lisa wished she knew some way to reassure him, but she wasn't any more certain than he was that the whole idea of the two of them starring together would even work.

They walked into the spacious lobby, and the first person Lisa saw was Drew Donovan. He stood with his back toward her, looking out a window across the room.

"When did Drew arrive?" Lisa hoped her voice sounded casual enough.

Tom's arm dropped from her shoulder and he studied her expression with what looked to be apprehension. "A couple of days ago. He wanted to get a feel for the place, he said, and familiarize himself with some of the filming locations. There's some rugged countryside we intend to use in the scenes when Conchita runs off with her renegade."

Lisa couldn't take her eyes off Drew. His broad shoulders and lean waist and hips had always appealed to her, and the casual shirt and well-worn jeans needlessly emphasized his masculine charm.

Drew must have heard their voices. He glanced around, then turned and strode toward them. Lisa studied his face, noting the slight changes. He appeared thinner and the lines around his mouth were deeper. Never had she seen his eyes without the special warmth they had always held for her. Now they looked cool and distant. He nodded politely to her, his face registering very little emotion.

"Hello, Lisa. I'm glad to see you made it all right."

She stood there staring at him, trying to drink him in all at once, after the twelve-month drought of not seeing him. He took her hand and squeezed it gently, which set up a tingling awareness of him that vibrated throughout her system.

"Hello, Drew."

Her voice was so soft that he almost didn't hear it. Her eyes seemed to fill her face, and he saw a sadness still lurking in their depths. A pain shot through him. She still hadn't gotten over losing their baby. He wondered if she ever would.

Someone called Tom, and he glanced around impatiently. Then he turned back to Drew. "Would you mind showing Lisa to her quarters, Drew? Things seem to be going to hell around here. I hope this isn't a sign of how the shooting's going to go." He looked first at one of them, then the other, as though waiting for some kind of reassurance. Neither one of them responded to the unspoken appeal. He shrugged and turned to Lisa. "I'll see you at dinner tonight to give you the schedule. It's going to be hectic, but no more than usual.'' He patted her on the shoulder, gave Drew a short wave and strode away.

Drew turned to Lisa, his voice carefully neutral. "You're down the hallway from me. We've both got rooms with a marvelous view. I'm sure you're going to enjoy it here."

Lisa decided he sounded like the hotel entertainment director, politely greeting a new arrival. But then, what had she expected? She wondered if he had brought anyone down here with him. In some ways, seeing him with someone else would make their time together easier. It would reinforce the reality of their situation as two people no longer on the same course. But she knew how much she dreaded to see him with someone else.

Humans are certainly irrational creatures, she thought with an inward smile. *How do I expect him to remarry and have a family if he doesn't get involved with someone else!*

Drew took Lisa's arm and gently propelled her down a long hallway. They left the main part of the hacienda. The corridor and guest rooms were obviously a more recent addition. They were filled with light and decorated with stately elegance. Lisa felt a slight lessening of tension. The place was so full of serenity and peace that some of it wafted around her, gently enfolding them.

The light scent of Drew's after-shave reached her and she shivered slightly. The memories evoked by the scent were better left unrecalled.

She had dreaded seeing Drew again. Well, now she had. Not knowing how he would treat her, she had imagined all sorts of things, but she needn't have worried. He was being distantly polite. Surely she could handle that.

"Here we are." Drew inserted the key Tom had handed him, opened the door and presented her with the key. She stepped inside and paused. The view of orchards and rolling hills gave a sense of timelessness to the place.

"Oh, Drew, this is—" She looked around but he hadn't followed her inside. She poked her head through the doorway in time to see another door closing down the hall. He hadn't waited. He'd done as Tom requested—no more and no less.

Lisa shook her head. *I wonder how we'll get through the next few weeks?*

Drew was asking himself the same question. He sank down on the edge of the bed, his knees trembling so he could scarcely stand. He'd just given the Oscar-winning performance of his life. Too bad no one had been around to appreciate it.

God, how he'd dreaded seeing her again. It had been worse than he'd expected. He should never have touched her, never felt the slight tremor in her hand, never felt the warmth of her arm beneath his fingertips when he guided her down the hall.

If he could only understand why she'd left. If he could only make some sense out of her change of attitude and feelings. Drew stretched out on the bed and tried to relax.

He'd known this was going to be a tough assignment, but he was determined to see it through. It would have been so much easier to give her the money, but he knew her pride wouldn't allow her to accept it. Too bad he couldn't tell her how much more painful it was for him to see her each and every day, to play opposite her in such a passionate love story, and know she wasn't interested in his love for her.

No. Lisa had no idea how much she was asking of him.

Lisa sat in front of her mirror, adding the finishing touches to her makeup. She'd carefully covered the signs of strain around her eyes and added more blush to her cheeks than she normally wore. Drew would not have cause to wonder at her lack of color. She intended to put on the performance of her career while in Mexico, and it wouldn't be in front of the cameras.

A slight knock at the door caused her to start, and she recognized how on edge she was. Tom had called earlier to say he would stop by her room to escort her to dinner. Grabbing her stole, she checked her clutch purse to make sure she had her room key, then opened the door. Tom's elfin grin greeted her.

"You look smashing, old girl. I always said red was your color."

"Actually, Tom, you manage to say that about everything I wear."

His grin widened. "So I do. That's because you look great in all the bold colors. No simpering pastels for you." He clasped her hand and started down the hallway.

"Are we eating alone tonight?"

He glanced over at her, his eyes only a few inches above hers. "Why? Are you afraid I'll make a pass at you?" His eyes danced with mischief.

With a slight chuckle, she shook her head. "As a matter of fact, the thought hadn't entered my mind. However..."

"Rest assured, milady, I have no evil designs on your luscious body, but you may be further reassured by the fact that I've reserved a room here so that all of us can eat together. I think it will be much more simple. We can cover a great deal of business over our meals that way."

"And encourage indigestion as well," she added wryly.

"How can you even suggest such a thing? Why, this picture is going to fall together like glue—there won't be any problems to cause indigestion."

"Could I have that guarantee in writing?" she asked with amused interest.

He grinned appreciatively. "Not likely. However, I really don't anticipate anything more than the usual irritating annoyances that occur whenever we're on location. Do you?"

Tom guided her through double doors to where several of the cast and crew were gathered enjoying predinner drinks. Drew stood by the makeshift bar listening intently to one of the cameramen. One of Drew's more endearing traits was his ability to focus on a person and listen to him, giving him his undivided attention.

Lisa recognized the abrupt relief she felt when she hadn't found him with another woman. It was one thing to accept something intellectually, but it was much more difficult to accept it emotionally. Perhaps this was what she'd needed, a chance to be around him without being a part of his life.

Drew knew the exact moment Lisa stepped through the door, her hand resting lightly on Tom's arm. He could feel himself tense at the picture they made, Tom so fair and slender, not much taller than Lisa, and Lisa, with her dark coloring and her flame-red dress, a perfect foil for him. Actually, any man looked better with Lisa on his arm.

He had no idea what Casey was saying to him but he nodded politely. He wondered how long he would wait before finding an excuse to join Tom and Lisa. He was going to make damn sure he sat with her at dinner.

Drew had made up his mind during the hours before dinner that he was going to do whatever he could to convince Lisa they needed to be together. He was operating in the dark, not understanding the reasons for the split, but he intended to convince her that she was wrong.

If Tom thought he was going to occupy her spare time while they were down there filming, he was in for quite a surprise.

Casey eventually wandered away to freshen his drink and Drew immediately joined the circle around Lisa. With prac-ticed ease he slid his arm around her waist and leaned down and kissed her near her ear. "Hello, darling. You look radiant tonight."

Drew's conversation stopper couldn't have been any more provocative. It wasn't so much his words, but his manner. His tone was possessive and seductive, and the look he gave her would have melted steel at twenty paces. Lisa was certain that everyone in the room had been waiting to see how they treated each other, what they said and how they behaved. Drew must have been just as aware of the spectators' curiosity as she was. So why had he done it?

She stood in the circle of Drew's arm, stunned at the change in the man since that afternoon. With a glance at the glass he held in his hand, she wondered how much he'd had to drink. Then she recognized that he was drinking ginger ale, a ploy both of them used, since neither drank except for an occasional glass of wine with dinner.

She stared up at him, bewildered. The chocolate-brown suit enhanced his tawny skin and caused his sherry-colored eyes to sparkle. Or was something else causing that gleam in his eyes? She shook her head slightly, as though dazed.

"You're certainly in a good mood tonight," she murmured.

"And why not? I'm looking forward to working on this movie—I think we're going to enjoy it, and the location is perfect for the story line." He glanced at Tom who was watching them with amused interest. "Was it planned that way?"

"As a matter of fact, I believe the writer *had* vacationed down here earlier and was quite taken with the place. When she talked to Adele about the screenplay, Lauraine suggested the Hacienda Vista Hermosa as a logical place to film."

Lisa could feel herself slowly relaxing against Drew. How many times over the years had they stood together in this very comfortable position? Drew was a toucher and she had quickly learned to enjoy the trait. It felt so natural and right to be in his arms again.

"Who is this Lauraine and why would she show her screenplay to Adele?" she asked.

Tom took a sip of his drink and cocked his head. "Adele is Lauraine Snelling's agent. As I understand it, Adele suggested she adapt her novel to a screenplay, and the rest, as they say, is history. Adele had no trouble selling the producer on the idea, especially when she suggested using you two in the leading roles."

Drew and Lisa stared at each other, then back at Tom. Lisa finally found her voice. "Are you saying that it was *Adele* who suggested Drew and me for this picture?"

Tom looked a little startled at the change in his female star. Why did she look so upset? "Well, uh, honestly, Lisa, I can't swear to it as fact. I just know when Harry called me he said he had a great screenplay and had been promised that the two of you would star in it, and I was as excited as he was about being part of the whole production." He glanced around at the small group listening to him. "I think we've got a smash hit on our hands, don't you?" he asked the group in general.

Drew stood there, thinking furiously about his conversation with Morey, and he had a strong hunch that he'd been had. He wondered why, and who was behind the whole setup. He leaned down and spoke in Lisa's ear in an undertone. "I think you and I have some talking to do."

Lisa remembered the scene in Adele's office. In particular she remembered Adele's insistence that both of them had to make the picture or neither would be offered the part. Was it possible that Adele had lied to her? After all these years, the knowledge that Adele could betray her caused her head to ache suddenly. *Oh, Adele, how could you?* she wondered.

What had Drew just said to her? Yes, they certainly did need to talk. Was it too late to back out of the picture? Adele would know. Adele. Lisa had always depended on Adele to handle the business end of her career. She'd relied on her integrity.

Tom didn't know what was going on, but he had a very bad feeling about it. Lisa was acting peculiar and he couldn't understand it. Her agent had pulled off the deal of the century. She'd found a promising writer, encouraged her to adapt her novel to the screen, had found a producer and managed to snag two of the biggest stars in the business. What was wrong with that?

He shrugged. Something, obviously. "C'mon, let's sit down and eat. I'm starving. How about you, love?" he asked Lisa as he took her hand and gently led her to one of the tables. Drew determinedly followed.

For some reason Lisa couldn't face Drew. After all, it had been her agent who'd pulled this despicable trick. She wasn't exactly sure how she'd done it, but by damn she was going to find out as soon as she got back to her room and the telephone.

Drew and Tom kept the conversation going, and Lisa forced herself to eat. She'd lost too much weight lately and knew if she didn't keep up her strength, she would become ill. There was no sense in adding to production costs because she was too selfish to take care of herself.

She was mentally counting how many more bites she needed to take when Drew said, "If it's all right with you, Tom, I'd like to take Lisa with me tomorrow. I want to take a ride out to the river and explore some of those caves we intend to use in the film.''

Tom raised his brows inquiringly at Lisa. ''Fine with me, but Lisa's the one to ask.''

''I know, but I wasn't sure when we're going to do the actual filming.''

''Well, Casey probably mentioned to you one of the crises that occurred this afternoon. A case of film wasn't what we ordered and we had to phone for more. Rather than start with what we have on hand, I thought I'd spend tomorrow with some of the crew members, setting up the key scenes we want to shoot first.'' He smiled at the two people sitting across from him. ''Since you'll be familiarizing yourself with the area, I think it's a good idea myself.'' He looked at Lisa. ''What do you think?''

What did she think? The swirling images parading through her mind could not possibly be classified as thoughts at the moment. She still hadn't recovered from what appeared to be Adele's treachery, nor from the shock of being with Drew again.

What did she think? About what? Somehow she must have missed the question. She stared at Drew, bewilderment plain on her face. He placed his hand over hers. "I thought I could rent a couple of horses. I know how much you enjoy riding."

No. She definitely didn't need to be reminded of other times with Drew, better times, happy times. But what excuse could she give? "If we don't go too far. It's been a while since I've done any riding." She avoided his gaze and turned her head toward Tom. "What is the shooting schedule, Tom?"

"Barring any more unforeseen events, I want to start Wednesday morning with the scene between Conchita and her father. Richard Driscoll is on a tight schedule and I promised to do all his scenes first."

Lisa knew they were fortunate to have coaxed the stage actor away from his first love, the theater, to play the role of her father. She was looking forward to meeting the man for the first time.

"I take it he hasn't arrived yet?" she asked.

"No. He's due in tomorrow evening and I hope will be prepared to start shooting right away."

"From everything I've heard about him," Drew pointed out, "he'll be fully prepared. He's quite a man."

Tom stood up. "You two enjoy your ride tomorrow, and I'll see you for dinner in the evening. Driscoll should be here by then."

Somewhat dismayed, Lisa watched Tom walk away. Did he intend to desert her just when she didn't want to be alone with Drew?

"Would you like to explain what you and Adele have been up to?" Drew asked in a soft tone of voice.

Lisa's gaze fell on Drew in amazement. "What Adele and I are up to? What are you talking about?"

"I'm talking about whoever told Morey that the producer wouldn't do this movie unless both of us were in it."

"That's exactly what Adele told me as well."

"How convenient for Adele. Her writer sells the screenplay, she gets a commission, she gets you a part in the movie, she gets a commission. I just don't understand how I came to be part of the deal.''

It was Lisa's turn to be confused. ''You mean you didn't want to do the movie? But I was told...'' Her voice dwindled away as she recalled her conversation with Adele.

''Yes. I'd like very much to learn what you were told.''

Did Drew need the money for this picture? If so, it was a carefully guarded secret and one she was not to admit knowing. Even discovering that Adele had possibly tricked her into agreeing to do the film, Lisa could not betray the confidence. After all, anyone could make a poor investment. It was nothing to be ashamed of, but Drew didn't need to discover she was aware of his problems.

She gazed up at him and smiled. ''Adele told me that the producer wanted both of us, or neither. I thought it was a marvelous story and agreed to do it. Why did *you* agree to do it?''

Drew stared down at Lisa's hands, loosely clasped on the table in front of her. Why had he agreed, really? Of course he knew why. Because he would do anything for this woman, anything at all. If she needed to do the movie, and she had just as much as admitted it, he would be there to help her.

He shrugged. "I thought it made a nice change of pace from some of my more recent films. I've gotten a little tired of the same old themes—life is real, life is earnest, and love is make-believe." His gaze returned to her face. "You see, I still believe in love, I believe in its power to change lives, to make each of us better people." He stroked his finger across her cheek. "And most of all, I believe in us—you and me. I wanted to see you again, Lisa. That's the honest-to-God truth. When I heard you were willing to do this picture with me, I jumped at the chance."

The look in his eyes turned her bones to overcooked noodles, and she almost sagged in her chair. *Please don't let him turn his full battery of charm on me. I can't deal with it,* she thought frantically. Hadn't he heard anything she said to him the day she'd left? How could he still want to see her and want to be around her? She could still see him standing in the hallway, pale and stricken, while she walked out on him. It could have happened yesterday, rather than almost a year ago. Surely he hadn't forgotten!

Hadn't he believed her? Was there some way he could sense her real feelings for him, despite her words? If so, she was lost because she couldn't possibly say them again, even at the ultimate cost of his happiness.

"Drew?" she finally whispered.

"Yes, love."

"I don't think this was a very good idea, our making the film together."

One side of his mouth lifted in a lopsided smile. "You're a little late in deciding that, I'm afraid."

She was afraid also. In fact, she was terrified. How was she going to hide her feelings for him if he treated her with so much love and kindness? She'd counted on his being hard and bitter, resenting her, even possibly snubbing her. Instead he was treating her as though nothing had happened to them, almost as though she'd never gotten pregnant and lost their child.

But she had and Lisa loved him too much to stand in the way of his eventually having a family of his own to love.

She stood up. "I'm rather tired," she said abruptly. "What time do you want to leave in the morning?"

Drew slowly came to his feet, puzzled at her sudden change of mood. He'd always been adept at reading her before, but she had changed too much during the past year. He hated that cold, aloof expression on her face, and he hoped he could discover how to erase it permanently.

"Why don't we meet for breakfast at eight, and leave right afterward."

"Fine. I'll see you in the coffee shop." Lisa grabbed her small purse and left the room as though all the hounds of hell were pursuing her. She felt as though they were.

She knew what the first thing she was going to do when she got to her room would be—and that was to call Adele. Her agent had some explaining to do!

Five

——

Lisa sat on the side of the bed, impatiently tapping her foot, while she listened to the endless ringing of the telephone. There was no answer at Adele's office or home, nor was there a recorder on either phone. What was Adele thinking of? She never left her phones unattended. In fact, she'd used an answering service for years, but had finally succumbed to the answering machine for messages.

Now what? Lisa returned the receiver to its cradle and stood up. She wished she could remember exactly how Adele had presented the script and the idea of her starring with Drew. All she could remember was her intense reaction to the thought of working with him again.

Whatever had possessed her to agree? One day around him and she could already feel herself slipping back into the old magic they seemed to share. She'd found herself hoping that Drew would suggest they spend some time together that night. Was she losing her mind? Any time spent with him only lowered her resistance to him. She didn't need that.

She lay in bed for a long time, watching the shadows traced on the wall beside her. Whenever she felt herself weakening, all she had to do was to remember the years she and Drew had dreamed and hoped and planned for their family. She could still picture the glowing anticipation on his face when he would talk about his dreams.

Why did life have to turn out like that? She would have done anything in her power to give him the family he wanted. Unfortunately, the only way she could do that was to bow out of his life completely.

Instead, she had agreed to come back into his life, at least on a temporary basis.

A thought suddenly occurred to her. She knew very well that Adele had said nothing about knowing the screenwriter. Was it possible she had also misled Lisa regarding Drew's need to make the film? What if that had been a fabrication? If so, she would never be able to forgive Adele.

Lisa's sleep was filled with restless dreams and swirling emotions. It was almost dawn before she fell into a deep sleep, which was why she didn't hear Drew's tap on her door the next morning.

Drew had looked for her in the coffee shop and had finally decided to check her room. He knew from experience what a sound sleeper she was and when he got no answer, went to the front desk and requested a key. Thank God the clerk knew they were married, although he probably thought it peculiar they weren't sharing a room. As a matter of fact, Drew had decided during a long, sleepless night to change that arrangement as soon as possible.

His gaze fell on the sleeping Lisa as soon as he opened the door. She slept on her side, one small hand tucked under her pillow, the other under her cheek. A slight frown creased her brow and he had the irresistible urge to smooth his hand across the delicate ridge. Her hair lay in tousled confusion around her face and shoulders, and Drew sank down on the side of the bed in the curl made by her body. He gently brushed the hair from her cheek.

"Lisa?"

She didn't stir.

"Darling, wake up."

There was no response.

A mischievous gleam appeared in Drew's eyes. He leaned down and began to kiss her, starting at her ear and following a trail along her cheek to her mouth.

She moaned and stirred slightly, shifting in the bed so that she now faced him. Almost unaware of his actions, Drew slipped his feet out of his shoes and stretched out on the bed beside her. The scene was blessedly familiar, but one he had never expected to share with her again. He pulled her into his arms and started kissing her.

Lisa was having the most delicious dream. She and Drew were together again and he was kissing her. No one kissed her the way Drew did. Or more to the point, she had never given anyone the opportunity to kiss her the way he did. Drew was very thorough in everything he did. Kissing her was no exception.

He was such a tease. Just when she thought he would find her lips he would move away, placing soft kisses on her eyelids, the tip of her nose. She tried to find his mouth with hers and she felt more than heard the soft laugh that was undeniably his.

"Don't tease me," she complained fretfully, her mouth searching for his.

His teasing had affected him, too, and when their mouths finally touched, searing sensation almost consumed them. They clung to each other, lost in the rediscovery of delightful responses.

Drew discovered he had unwittingly hampered himself by stretching out on top of the covers that so demurely covered Lisa. He held her so closely to him that the sheet provided an excellent shield from his exploring hand.

Lisa's dream seemed so real. She could almost feel the silkiness of his hair as she ran her fingers through it, smell the tantalizing scent of his after-shave, hear the harsh sound of his breathing. . . .

Her eyes fluttered open and she realized she wasn't dreaming.

"Drew?" she whispered. What was he doing in bed with her? Her fogged brain tried to recall recent events. She hadn't been able to sleep; then when she'd finally fallen asleep she'd dreamed. "Drew!" She sat up, ineffectually pushing him away. "What are you doing in here?"

He grinned. "What's it look like I'm doing? Trying to wake up my wife."

She didn't need the reminder that they were still married. Nor did she need the reminder of what it was like to wake up in his arms. It had taken her months to get used to sleeping without him. She tried to move away from him but his weight on the covers kept her pinned to his side.

"Would you get off this bed," she muttered, "so that I can get up?"

"Certainly." He nimbly got to his feet and gave her a graceful bow. A Spanish don could not have done it better.

She started to throw the covers back, then thought better of the idea. The nightgown she wore left little to the imagination. It was one of many that Drew had personally chosen for her to wear. Of course he'd seen her in it before, but she had to keep some distance between them, or at the very least start putting some between them immediately, or she would be in big trouble.

"I'm awake now, Drew. I'm sorry I overslept. Why don't you go ahead and order breakfast. I'll be there by the time it arrives."

"I'll be glad to help you get ready, love. Surely you remember how good I am at scrubbing your back in the shower." His eyes had an unholy gleam in them that told her he knew how she was reacting to his presence.

She reached for her robe and drew it around her shoulders. Trying hard to ignore him, she stood up and headed for the bathroom. "Yes, I do. Somehow I'll just have to manage without you." She paused at the bathroom door. "Goodbye, Drew," she stated firmly.

He wondered if she knew how sheer her robe was and that the sight of her silhouetted in the doorway had a very strong effect on him. He wondered if she even cared and that thought gave him pause.

Whether he liked it or not, they were separated because she'd made it clear she didn't want to live with him, or be around him. Oh, yes, she'd made that almost brutally clear. How easy it was for him to pretend that none of that had really happened. But it had. He'd had twelve months to live with the knowledge and try to come to terms with it.

Would he ever reach that point?

Lisa watched the teasing expression disappear from Drew's face. The hard lines she'd first noticed the day before settled across his countenance and he nodded. "All right. I'll see you in about twenty minutes, if you think that will give you enough time."

"Yes, thank you."

She watched him open the door and step out of the room, closing the door quietly behind him. For a little while he'd been the Drew she'd known, loved and married. She wasn't at all sure she could deal with or understand the new, harsher Drew.

Is that what her leaving had done to him? She flinched at the thought. Pinning her hair up, Lisa quickly stepped into the shower, almost afraid to pursue her thoughts.

When Lisa paused in the doorway of the coffee shop Drew immediately stood up and briskly walked over to her, escorting her to their table.

"Do you still have fruit and toast for breakfast?" he asked in a quiet tone.

She nodded, unable to respond verbally. He looked so good to her—that special freshly scrubbed look that seemed to burnish his golden tan with light. The scent of his after-shave continued to haunt her, and the burning light in his eyes made her feel as though it singed the surface of her skin. How in the world were they going to work together?

"I don't think this was such a good idea," Lisa finally murmured after she sat her coffee cup back into the saucer.

"What? Having breakfast together or taking a ride together?"

"Both. And making a movie together."

He raised one brow in a slightly quizzical look. "But I thought it was all your idea, our making a movie together."

"Of course it wasn't! I tried to explain to you last night. I understood the only reason the movie was being made was for us to be in it together. I didn't want to knock you out of making it."

His grin was not one of amusement. "You're all heart, Lisa. However, I could quit making pictures today and never have to worry about my income."

Was he telling her the truth or trying to make light of his current financial situation?

"Perhaps we should call it off, then," she offered, wondering why her heart pounded in her chest at the thought. Was it relief or dread at the proposal?

"It's too late, my love. We both signed contracts. Whether we like it or not, we're stuck together for the duration." He straightened in his chair slightly. "One of the reasons I wanted us to take a ride was to face what it's going to mean to us to work together for the next several weeks, and to decide the best way to get through it with minimum pain on either side."

Lisa took the last bite of her fruit, chewing slowly.

Drew continued. "It may be the last time we have a chance to be alone. The schedule is hectic, which is understandable. The longer we stay, the more expensive the overhead. In our case, the sooner the film is completed, the quicker we can get on with our lives."

"Then you're agreeing to the divorce?"

"I didn't say that. I don't believe I even implied it, but I can see that the divorce is uppermost in your mind. I had hoped we could talk about your reasons for wanting one and perhaps see if there were alternative avenues we could consider." Drew glanced at her empty plate and smiled. "Are you ready to go?"

Lisa was amazed to discover she'd eaten everything placed in front of her when she'd been convinced she wouldn't be able to eat a bite. She nodded and watched Drew stand up in his lithe, graceful way and pull her chair out for her.

"I can't remember the last time I was on horseback," she said, trying to keep the conversation casual during their walk to the stables.

"I can," he said with a grin. "Remember when we decided to camp in southern Arizona and rented those horses? You swore you wouldn't get near one again."

"How could I forget? But that was because my horse didn't like me!"

"Why should he? If I'd been labeled with as many names as you gave him in only two days, I wouldn't have cared for you myself."

Lisa grinned, remembering the trip, the fun and laughter they'd shared, and the delightful lovemaking. She seemed to exist on memories these days, and all of them brought at least a twinge of pain.

Their horses were saddled and waiting for them, and before too long Drew was leading her away from the hacienda. The gently rolling hills were appealing, and she wished she could concentrate on them. Instead, her eyes kept returning to the path in front of her while she filled her senses with new visions of Drew.

His hair had grown longer, so that the wave was more noticeable and when he turned his head she could see how it curled around his ears, the tawniness glowing in the sunlight. His shoulders seemed even wider than she'd remembered, and her fingers tingled with the memory of touching the rippling muscles that caused his shirt to cling to his body. The warmth of the sun had caused a slight darkening along his spine where moisture was beginning to collect, causing his shirt to mold itself to the contours of his back.

His waist and hips were small for a man his size and height, and she recalled teasing him about his snake hips. Drew seemed totally unaware of his looks and their effect on everyone around him. Although Lisa knew that his looks had been the first thing she'd noticed about him, it had been his personality, his wonderful love for life and all it had to offer that quickly endeared him to her. His lack of pretension, his inquiring mind, his eagerness to learn more about everything, had caused her to quickly succumb to the power of his presence.

She shook her head, trying to distract herself from her thoughts. It did no good to dwell on him. What she needed to remember was the necessity to maintain a distance from him and continue to convince him that she wanted to be free of him.

She was an actress—a darned good actress—and she was determined to portray a woman who'd fallen out of love and no longer wanted a marriage. It would be the greatest acting assignment of her career. And the most heartbreaking.

Drew eventually paused by a river that danced merrily through the countryside. After dismounting, he walked over to her and held up his arms. "We'd better rest awhile before starting back. I don't want that delicious backside of yours to complain of my inhuman treatment of you."

Lisa could feel the color spring into her cheeks. She'd forgotten Drew's ability to say the unpredictable and once again he'd caught her off guard. He'd always teased her about the alluring shape of her hips and sworn that he fell in love with her the first time she'd turned her back on him and haughtily stalked away.

Lisa placed her hands on his shoulders and leaned into him, her horse patiently waiting for her to dismount. He lifted her slight weight easily from her horse, then let her slowly slide down the long length of him. Not fair. Not fair at all.

The problem was that he knew her too well. He knew how much he affected her and how little control she seemed to have over her own reactions when he was around. Today was no different. By the time he stepped politely away from her, Lisa could scarcely breathe.

After allowing the horses to drink, they tied the reins around a sturdy bush and without speaking began to follow the river upstream. Drew watched for rough spots and on more than one occasion grasped her hand to help her, only to politely let go when they were past the difficult area.

Lisa wished she knew what he was thinking. When had he acquired the ability to hide his feelings and thoughts from her? At one time he'd seemed so open and loving, and she'd felt as though there could never come a time when she'd be shut out of his thoughts.

"Do you want to stop and rest?" he asked when they came upon a grassy verge.

The hot sun had created tiny rivulets of perspiration that trickled between her breasts and beaded her brow. "That's the best idea you've had all day," she admitted breathlessly, sinking down beside the river with a quick sigh of relief. She began to tug at her riding boots, gratefully peeling off her socks until she could dangle her feet in the cool water.

Drew sat down beside her. "Actually," he drawled, "I've had much better ideas but I didn't think you'd go for them."

Lisa pushed her hair back from her face, wishing she'd thought to braid it before coming on this ride. She could feel the stickiness on the back of her neck. "What sort of ideas?" she asked with suspicion.

He studied her face with a slight smile. "Never mind." He glanced over the river. "We could always go swimming."

"I didn't bring a suit."

"I know," he murmured, still staring out over the river.

"I don't think it would be a good idea for us to swim without them," she muttered.

"I know," he agreed indifferently.

She wished he hadn't mentioned it because the idea had considerable merit. It wasn't as though they hadn't done it many times before. However, she could remember quite well how all of those swimming episodes had ended. Neither one of them wanted that to happen now. Or did she?

Lisa didn't know whether it was the heat or her provocative thoughts that caused her to squirm, but she jerked her feet out of the water and stood up. "I think we'd better get back, don't you?"

Drew had stretched out on the grass, looking for all the world as if he'd found a home. "Why?"

"It will be lunchtime when we return."

He glanced over at his horse, which was placidly chewing on the succulent grass. "I brought food in the saddlebags."

"Oh."

She needed to put her socks and boots back on, but she hesitated. The water had cooled them off and she knew the boots would be hot. But she couldn't walk around barefoot.

Lisa slowly sank down beside Drew once again. "What did you bring?"

"I don't know. I know what I ordered. Arturo was to see that it was packed, but I haven't checked it." He glanced at her under his long lashes. "Why? Are you hungry?"

Of course she wasn't hungry. She was nervous, and the longer she stayed alone with Drew, the more nervous she was going to be. Why did she have the feeling he was well aware of that fact?

"A little." Liar.

"Are you sure you don't want to go swimming?"

"Positive."

"Would you mind if I go in?"

Of course I'd mind! Do you think I'm made of stone? "Not at all," she managed to murmur in a distant tone.

"Great!" he said, sitting up and grabbing at his shirt. He peeled it off and his glistening chest beckoned to her, the heavy muscles daring her to trace them. She turned her head and stared across the river while he continued to undress beside her. The movements beside her tugged at her attention, and she had to fixedly concentrate on the view in front of her and not let her imagination remind her of what he was doing.

When she heard the splash Lisa assumed it was all right to look. However, the water was only thigh-deep on Drew and his well-developed buttocks shone briefly, then were covered by his next step into deeper water. Lisa forcibly took a deep breath and exhaled slowly.

Drew took several strokes until he was almost in the center of the river where the water ran with a lazy current. "Wow, this is great. Sure you don't want to try it?" he asked with a grin.

"Positive." She forced herself to lie down. "I think I'll take a quick nap. Wake me up when you're ready to eat."

She heard his laugh and a certain amount of unnecessary splashing while she determinedly closed her eyes and tried to find some tranquil thoughts to dwell on. She needed to think of anything but Drew's nude body that was only a few feet away from her.

Unfortunately most of her thoughts were about Drew and about other instances when she had seen him in that condition—climbing out of the hot tub on the deck of their home, casually grabbing a towel and wrapping it around his loins; strolling out of the bathroom after a shower, finding her still in the bedroom and catching her unaware, grabbing her and falling on the bed with her in his arms.

Lisa's eyes flew open, her thoughts determined to betray her firm resolve. Drew was still in the water, swimming leisurely, obviously enjoying himself. She felt the perspiration continuing to trickle down her back and between her breasts. Why was she punishing herself? What was wrong with enjoying the coolness of the water? She stared at the blue sky for an answer but none came.

Slowly, Lisa sat up. Drew was downstream from her, facing the other way. Hesitantly she reached for the top button of her blouse, then with sudden determination, her decision made, she hurriedly stripped away her confining clothing and stood up. The breeze felt good on her overheated body. She slipped her legs into the wonderfully cool water and waded toward the middle of the river. It no longer mattered to her that Drew might see her, or that her hair would be a mess. Comfort came first and the water was a blessing on her warm skin, answering a promise of surcease from the sun and her thoughts.

She started swimming upstream with firm, rapid strokes, diving briefly underwater, then raising her head, forcing her hair away from her face.

Drew had been right—the water was wonderful.

"Couldn't resist, could you?"

Startled at the closeness of his voice, Lisa lost the rhythm of her stroke and water splashed into her mouth. She choked, looking around her. Drew was easily pacing her in the water, his eyes dancing above the crystal clarity of the river.

"You scared me!" she accused when she could get her breath.

He turned over, floating. "How could I scare you, love? You knew I was here."

She quit swimming and began to tread water. The water was so clear that she could see his entire body spread in front of her. "I thought you were swimming downstream."

"So you decided to come upstream. How terribly modest of you," he drawled. "Are you by chance concerned that I might have evil designs upon your enticing body?"

"Don't be silly." Lisa began to swim in a diagonal line toward the shore, where she had left her clothes.

Drew obligingly paced her. "You know I've always enjoyed getting my hands on your luscious body, Lisa. Why call it silly?"

Without looking at him she pulled herself up on the bank and began to wring her hair out. Of course she wasn't self-conscious in front of Drew. How could she be? He knew her body as well as, if not better than, she did. He certainly knew every place on her body that could respond to him. Lisa hoped he wouldn't take advantage of that fact. She was too vulnerable to him now.

Drew pulled himself out of the river and sat down a few feet away. "That was great, wasn't it?"

Lisa glanced around, her gaze tracing the rivulets of water that slithered down his chest. Forcing her gaze to meet his, she nodded. "Yes, it was. Thank you for suggesting it."

He stood up and stretched, and the sunlight glinted off his golden skin. "My pleasure." He leaned over and picked up his shirt, tossing it to her. "Here—you can use this for a towel."

Grateful for his casual tone and manner, Lisa caught the shirt and hastily dried herself. With jerky movements she pulled her clothes back on. By the time she was dressed

Drew had laid out the food that Arturo had packed for them. The meal consisted of hearty sandwiches, fruit and bottled water, and Lisa was surprised at her appetite.

"Are you ready to go back?" Drew asked after they had eaten. Lisa felt relaxed by the peacefulness that had settled around them while they ate and enjoyed the view. Drew had the uncanny ability to make her relax, even when he was the one with whom she most needed to keep up her guard. But for some reason she felt no more pressure from him. For this small moment in time they had unconsciously agreed to enjoy the chance to be together, without questioning the past or the future. It was enough for them to have the present.

Lisa sighed. "Yes. We'd better get back before someone starts to worry."

Drew smiled. "It wouldn't do for the stars of the film to get lost the day before shooting begins, now would it?"

"I was surprised at how easily Tom agreed for us to go," she admitted.

"I wasn't," Drew replied with a grin. "Tom has let me do all the exploring I want. He knows I've been too restless to stay cooped up at the hacienda, despite the distractions offered."

Lisa was well aware of the distractions— the lovely women she'd seen, their black eyes flashing impishly. She was in total agreement with Tom, even though she had to admit her jealousy was irrational and totally illogical. Since she fully intended to divorce Drew so that he could remarry someone who could have his children, she wasn't making much sense by preferring he be alone.

Drew walked to her side to help her into the saddle. He placed his hands on her waist and gripped firmly. "I've enjoyed today with you, Lisa. Thank you." He leaned down and kissed her softly.

She could feel the tautness in his body, feel the leashed energy within him so tightly under control. "I enjoyed it, too, Drew," she whispered. "Thank you."

Lisa turned toward her mount, and Drew boosted her into the saddle. They rode back to the hacienda in silence, each caught up in his and her own thoughts—once again trapped between the past, the present and the unpredictable future.

Six

"Now...in this scene Conchita's father has announced to the family that he and a neighboring landowner have entered into an agreement for their son and daughter to marry." Tom glanced around at the assembled cast. "We're shooting this scene now because Richard Driscoll has to return to New York by the weekend. The next scene will be the confrontation between Richard and Lisa. I'd like to get these two scenes wrapped up today." Once again he glanced around. "Are there any questions?"

Lisa watched the faces of the assembled actresses and actors. All of them were good at their jobs and they were ready to shoot. Rehearsals had gone smoothly, and Lisa felt a glow deep within her. This film was going to be good. There was a current running among all of them, encouraging an intense response to one another. Sometimes a good director could cause such a closeness in a group, but generally it took weeks of working together to reach this stage. For some reason, by the third day of rehearsals, the small cast had pulled together, bolstering one another to do better than their best.

Lisa glanced around, unconsciously looking for Drew, but he wasn't there. She hadn't seen him for three days, except during their evening meals, which everyone shared. Of course she'd been busy rehearsing scenes that he had no part in, so there was no reason to look for him. But she had.

That was the insidious thing about a relationship such as theirs. They each seemed to be such a part of each other that she felt as though something was missing when he wasn't around. Her heart, perhaps?

"All right, everybody," Tom concluded. "Let's get started."

The smooth, famous tones of Richard Driscoll flowed over her. "You are looking delightfully buxom in that dress, my dear. How do they ever expect me to pretend you're my daughter, expecting filial devotion from you, when my natural instincts will be to throw you on the nearest sofa and ravish you?" The twinkling blue eyes belied the ferocious frown and grim smile, and Lisa burst out laughing.

"Richard, you've been a joy to work with, and I'm going to miss you terribly. Your outrageous comments and suggestions have been terrific for my ego."

"Your ego may have been boosted, but being around you has played hell with my libido, let me assure you. I've only been *cast* as your father. There's been no reason to treat me as one off the set, you know."

"And exactly what would you have done differently had I taken you up on any of your outlandish suggestions, my friend?"

"Outlandish? How can you say that?"

"Easy. We would both have to be gold medal gymnasts to perform some of the suggestions you've made."

He grinned, the famous, heartwarming grin that endeared him to women around the world. "So we would. Then maybe it's just as well you exerted some control over our love affair."

"How can we be having a love affair when we've never even touched each other?"

"That question proves to me how little you know about human nature. We have touched on the most intimate level—our minds. We have met and shared ourselves as few people have been able to do. And because of that, I will love you forever."

His tone had dropped, and she stared at him because the actor had disappeared and only the man stood before her. Richard Driscoll was in his early fifties but it didn't show. He still played the leading man with panache and heart-stirring sensuality, so that his agreeing to play the part of her father had come as a surprise to many. He was slim and dark, a perfect choice for the don of the hacienda in looks, with a commanding air that radiated from him. Lisa stared into his eyes, witnessing the sincerity in them, recognizing the truth of what he'd just said. They had instantly treated each other like old friends who had been parted for years, eager to catch up on each other's life.

He had told her about some of the more painful periods of his life, sharing the heartache, the more joyous periods and the laughter. She had done the same.

She had even told him how she had suffered when she lost the baby and later left Drew. He had never asked questions, only listened thoughtfully, intently and without judgment. He was right. They had become intimate friends in a very short time, and she knew she was going to miss him.

Richard took her hand. "I want to stay in touch, Lisa. Let me know how you're doing and if there is anything I can do for you. You are a very beautiful person and you deserve happiness. I'm still hoping you'll be able to find it with Drew."

Lisa withdrew her hand. "That's impossible, Richard, but I appreciate your thoughtfulness.'' They stood in the large lounge of the hacienda, waiting for Tom to cue them for their scene. Lisa glanced around for Tom, and her gaze met Drew's furious one. How long had he been there, and why did he look so angry?

"Places, everybody," Tom called. "Richard, let wardrobe look at your left sleeve. The lace seems to have come unstitched. Lisa, take a seat in the burgundy-colored sofa, next to your mother. Your sister will be in the chair next to you."

She sat down next to Estelle and absently smiled a greeting while her eyes searched once again for Drew. He was still there, standing on the sidelines in a deceptively casual pose, his shoulder leaning against a pillar. She could feel the anger radiating all around him and she wondered why.

Then the scene began and Lisa had no time to think about anything but the job at hand.

Lisa wearily opened the door to her room, grateful to have the day behind her. It was after six and she needed to shower and dress for dinner. But for the moment all she could think about was the need to lie down. With a sigh, she slipped off her shoes and stretched across the bed.

Both the scenes shot today had been draining. In the first one she'd had to react to the news of a betrothal with a man she had no respect for and knew she could never love. The second one, in which she carried most of the lines, she'd had to initiate the scene between her and her father when she explained that she had not been kidnapped by Reynaldo, but had run away with him, that she had slept with him, expected his child and would return to him whenever she could.

The problem with filming out of sequence was the necessity to prepare for each scene separately. During the run of a play, the story line became a part of the actor and tension began to build toward the climax, flowing naturally and freely into a confrontation. Filming out of sequence meant she had to force the emotional intensity from her own inner resources rather than use the momentum gained from a previous scene.

However, the important thing to remember was that both scenes were now completed. There was only one scene left to do with Richard and then he could return to New York. She had reason to feel blessed that he had chosen to do the film with her. Whenever two established actors had a scene together, it sometimes became a contest between the two as to who would dominate. Not so in today's filming. Richard had undoubtedly been the focal point during the first scene and he could easily have upstaged her during the second scene had he so desired. Instead he played to her, his reactions enhancing her own, his superb acting abilities bringing out the very best she had. Lisa had even surprised herself and after Tom had declared the scene to be over, Lisa had received a round of applause from those watching the filming. Richard had joined in, as well.

It was days like today that made her chosen career worth while, but so few people understood the toll such a scene took on a person. Lisa felt as though all her emotions had been yanked from her, twisted and turned, manipulated and torn, and she felt drained.

She toyed with the idea of having a meal sent to her room but knew that was the coward's way out. It was more than tiredness that made her want to skip the gathering of the group tonight. Although she hadn't seen Drew since they'd started filming, she was still very aware of the anger she'd sensed in him earlier that morning, and she wasn't at all sure she was ready to deal with it. Lisa wasn't certain why she knew the anger had been directed at her. She just did.

Sometime later the shrill ringing of the phone next to the bed jarred her into wakefulness, and Lisa groped for the offending instrument.

"Do you intend to eat tonight?" demanded Drew in a harsh tone.

The room was dark, and Lisa fumbled for the lamp switch. "What time is it?"

"A little past eight."

They generally all met at seven-thirty for drinks. "I'm sorry. I must have been more tired than I thought. I'll be there in fifteen minutes."

There was a pause, then Drew offered, "Would you like me to have something sent to your room?"

The idea sounded heavenly. "Oh, Drew, that would be marvelous."

"When?"

"Oh, give me about twenty minutes."

"Fine."

Lisa heard the click as the line disconnected, and she hung up, too. Whatever had been bothering Drew still seemed to be in the air, but she would have to face him another day. She felt disoriented and groggy and wondered if she'd have the energy to eat.

Sitting up, she began to pull her clothes off and, after searching for a nightgown, she grabbed her robe and headed into the bathroom.

Lisa was blowing her hair dry when she heard the knock at the door. The timing was perfect. She hoped Drew hadn't ordered anything heavy because she intended to go back to bed as soon as she'd finished eating.

"Just a minute," she called, making sure her robe was securely tied before opening the door. A smiling waiter with a covered tray on a rolling cart stood outside. When she beckoned him in she noticed he wasn't alone. Drew walked in behind him.

"I took the liberty of ordering a meal for two. I wasn't really looking forward to the noise and chatter of our shared dining room tonight."

Lisa smiled faintly and turned away. "So long as you don't mind that I'm going to be poor company tonight. I'm really tired."

"Tom tells me you did a fantastic job today and is already predicting another Academy Award nomination."

Lisa chuckled. "That sounds like Tom. Eagerly optimistic."

"I'm sorry I missed it." Drew stuck his hands in the back pockets of his snug-fitting Levi's and wandered over to the window.

Lisa watched the waiter efficiently set the small table near the windows and gave him a tip as he left, for which she received a radiant smile and a quiet, *"Gracias."*

"I didn't think I was hungry," she said to Drew's back, "but you managed to order all my favorites. I'm surprised you remembered."

Drew came over to the table and pulled out her chair for Lisa, then sat down opposite her. His intent gaze seemed to pierce her when he said, "I've never forgotten anything about you, Lisa—your likes, dislikes, your laugh, your smile, the way you fit into my arms as though you were made for them, the way you respond to me when I'm loving you—I carry it all with me wherever I go."

Lisa sat across from him, holding herself very still, for fear she'd shatter in a thousand pieces if she should so much as shift her weight. The force of Drew's feelings pinned her into immobility. Before she could find any words to respond, Drew continued.

"I've tried to give you the time you needed to come to terms with the loss of our baby. I've tried to understand your need to leave me—I assumed I was too much of a reminder—but Lisa, I need you too much to allow you to end what we have together without at least trying to find alternatives to your solution."

Lisa could not look into his eyes any longer, and she picked up her fork and began to eat the delicate shrimp arranged in the salad before her. She didn't want to hear what he had to say because she'd gone over it in her own mind, time and time again, trying to figure another way out of the dilemma.

She had even considered telling Drew the truth, but was afraid he would deny his innermost feelings and insist that their inability to have children together did not matter, a lie that both of them would be forced to live.

Because it did matter—she knew it did. A family was one of Drew's most fervent goals, although he had been patient about the timing, waiting for their careers to stabilize so that both of them would have the necessary time to spend with a family. Neither of them had wanted someone else raising their family.

As much as she loved Drew, she was afraid he wouldn't face what the news meant to their future until it was too late and he had become bitter because of what she had denied him. The doctor had assured her that Drew would be able to father normal children with someone else—just not with her.

After the grueling day she'd had, Lisa would have preferred postponing this conversation, but it seemed inevitable, and she decided she might as well get on with it.

"Drew—" she spoke his name softly, very tenderly, and with an underlying sadness "—we always said that we would never hold on if a time came in our relationship when the other one wanted out. We both recognized that there are many people in the world and you and I are exposed to the most beautiful, the most handsome, the most talented, and that someday we might meet another person that would mean more to us than what we shared—and in that event, we would understand and let the other go free."

The lines in Drew's face grew deeper as he searched her face. Lisa determinedly returned his stare with a calm she was far from feeling. What if he called her bluff?

He did. "Is that why Richard Driscoll was willing to take time out from his busy schedule to do this part with you?"

Startled at the mention of Richard's name, Lisa could only stare at him, perplexed.

"It's obvious there's something between the two of you. The set seemed electrically charged whenever the two of you were together."

"Drew, you can't be serious. Richard is very much in love with his wife of twenty-five years."

The bitterness in his face made her cringe inside. "That may be true, but it doesn't mean he doesn't appreciate all you have to offer."

"You're wrong. Very wrong."

Drew picked up his glass of wine and sipped from it. Staring into the clear liquid as though reading a crystal ball, he asked, "If it isn't Richard, then who is it?"

"What's important now, Drew, is that it isn't you," she offered quietly.

His expression remained impassive while Drew continued to stare into his wineglass, but his knuckles whitened as he gripped the glass until the delicate stem shattered in his hand.

They sat for a moment in shock, staring at the remains of the glass, then Lisa took the broken glass and ran to the bathroom, tossing the liquid in the sink and grabbing a towel to wrap around his hand.

Drew took the towel without speaking, carefully brushing the sparkling pieces of glass into a neat pile on the linen tablecloth. Luckily none of the cuts on his palm were deep, and he strode into the bathroom and closed the door.

Lisa could hear the water running, and she glanced at the table with dismay. Their meal could not be considered a success—of that she was certain. She had hurt Drew again, and she could feel his pain as though it were her own. But she didn't know what else to do.

The bathroom door opened and she spun around, watching him anxiously.

A rueful smile appeared on Drew's face. "That might be considered dramatic in a movie scene, but I feel like an absolute fool."

A sweeping rush of relief ran through her when she realized he was trying to lighten the atmosphere. She moved toward him. "How's your hand?"

He held it out to her. "Actually, I've had worse cuts shaving in the morning, but if you want to kiss it to make it better, be my guest." There was a slight note of teasing in his tone that Lisa found reassuring.

"Oh, that won't be necessary, but I don't think you want to try to eat, for fear of getting a piece of glass."

Drew glanced at the table and shrugged. "Oh, I don't know. Ground-up glass might be just what I need."

"Not funny, I'm afraid."

He looked down at her and saw the signs of hastily dashed away tears, and Drew acknowledged to himself that he was making a melodrama of something that happened between married couples all the time. Just because they'd had several good years of married life together didn't mean they had a guarantee of continued marital bliss. So why had he always thought he and Lisa were the exception?

Cupping his uncut hand along her cheek, he said, "I'm sorry, baby. Sorry for barging in here tonight, sorry for trying to badger you into changing your mind, sorry it didn't work out between us." He stepped back, away from her soft scent that brought back so many memories. He had to quit living in the past. "I'm not going to fight you anymore, love. I want you to be happy and if I can't provide that happiness for you, I hope you'll find it somewhere else."

Drew opened the door to the hallway and looked back at her. Never had she looked more beautiful, her midnight black hair framing her delicate face, the soft peach of her satin robe echoed in the tint of her cheeks, her eyes huge in her face. "I won't fight you about the divorce, Lisa." He closed the door quietly behind him.

Lisa stood in the center of her room, staring at the door. She had done it. He was finally beginning to accept their separation.

She was relieved. Of course she was. She'd waited almost a year for this moment. It was a success of sorts. Then why was she standing there in the middle of a luxurious hotel room with tears streaming down her face? Why did she feel such an emptiness inside, knowing she'd never find another person whom she would be able to love as she did Drew?

Lisa had made the right decision. All she had to do now was to live with it.

Seven

———

The next morning Lisa caught a glimpse of her pale face and puffy eyes in the bathroom mirror and decided that the makeup department would certainly earn their pay today.

The scenes to be filmed that day would portray Conchita as lighthearted and gay. Lisa stood under the shower and tried to prepare herself for the role.

Lighthearted and gay. When had she felt lighthearted and gay?

Their wedding and honeymoon. She would never forget. They had decided to get married in her hometown so that her family could be present. It was a small ceremony, private and very beautiful. Drew made arrangements for them to fly to Missouri in a private plane because he didn't want publicity about their sudden marriage.

Her family had welcomed Drew into their hearts and homes and he'd been treated to several stories about the misadventures of Lisa as a child.

"I'm never going to see you as tiny and helpless again, you know," Drew told her the evening before the wedding. "According to your brothers, you were a holy terror and kept them all at bay."

They had followed a trail into the woods behind her parents' farm.

"I never pretended to be helpless. And I have no control over my size," Lisa replied with wounded dignity.

"Did you really try to jump off the barn loft holding an umbrella?"

"Mary Poppins never had a problem."

"Oh, Lisa." He stopped her by pulling her into his arms. "I love you so much. It scares me to think I might not have found you."

She went up on her toes, loving the feel of his body pressed so close against her. He picked her up in his arms and his mouth found hers in a searing kiss.

"How can I go to sleep tonight without you in my arms," he finally whispered, when he could find his breath.

"I'm sure one of my nieces would be pleased to loan you a teddy bear, if that would help."

He laughed. "I think I'll pass. Instead, I'll lie there tonight and think of all the things I intend to do tomorrow night, after you've become Mrs. Drew Donovan."

Lisa nuzzled his ear. "I can hardly wait."

"Did your folks say anything about our getting married so soon after we met?"

"They knew better. My folks had only known each other three weeks when they ran off and got married."

Drew let her slide down him slowly, intimately, until her shoes touched the ground once more.

"How long have they been married?"

"Thirty-eight years."

They turned around and started back to the house. "I'm looking forward to our thirty-eighth anniversary some day, with all our children and grandchildren gathered around." Drew paused outside the house and stared up at the sky for several minutes without speaking. "I no longer feel alone in the world, Lisa. With you in my life, I'll never be alone again."

Twenty-four hours later Drew and Lisa stood on the clean white beach of a small island in the South Pacific.

"It's so beautiful here, it doesn't seem real," Lisa said quietly. The moon shone so brightly that they needed no other light, and Lisa could see the silhouette of the palm trees as they leaned gracefully toward the sea. "I feel like the last few days have been a dream."

They had arrived by private jet less than an hour before. Drew had kept their destination a secret, and Lisa was delighted with his choice of a place to spend their first weeks together alone. They had found their own private paradise.

"Are we the only ones on the island?"

"Not quite. The island is privately owned, but there's a small settlement on the other side. The place is surprisingly self-sufficient." He ran his hand along the length of Lisa's spine. "Could I interest you in a tour of the place we'll call home for the next two weeks?"

His eyes glinted in the moonlight and she saw the flash of his smile.

"By all means," she said with dignity, then ruined it with "I'll race you," and took off running. By the time they reached the steps, they were both breathless.

Lisa paused in the doorway, but Drew scooped her up into his arms and strode with determination toward the bedroom.

"You don't appear to be hampered by jet lag," Lisa pointed out as he lowered her to the bed.

"Not yet, anyway," he agreed. "I'm not making any guarantees about how I'll feel tomorrow, though." He leaned over her. "Would you care to take a shower with me?" he asked, kissing her lightly on the nose.

"Um-hmm."

Before she could get up, Drew picked her up again and walked into the large adjoining bathroom.

"I'm perfectly capable of walking, Drew. Marriage hasn't made me helpless, you know."

He began to undress her. "I know, but I enjoy it. Humor me." He reached inside the tub and turned on the shower, then removed his clothing with economical movements.

As soon as they stepped into the tub, Drew picked up a bar of soap and began to make lather. With a serious expression on his face he drew circles and other geometric designs on Lisa with the foam. "This is much more fun than finger painting on paper," he explained solemnly.

She took the soap away from him and embarked on some artistic designs of her own. By the time they got out of the shower Lisa was weak with laughter.

Drew was outrageous, preposterous and more fun than anyone she had ever known.

He lay stretched out on the bed beside her, propped up on one elbow, his head resting on his hand, obviously enjoying the view of her unclothed body.

"Aren't you going to turn out the light?" she asked a little breathlessly.

"Uh-uh. I want to see you." He slowly traced a line with his hand from her throat downward, between her breasts, to the rounded indentation of her navel, then paused to ask, "Am I keeping you awake?"

"You certainly are. I've never felt less sleepy in my life!"

He traced the same path once again, this time with his lips. "Good," she heard him say. "Are you ready for your next lesson in lovemaking?"

The things that he was doing to her body should be outlawed, Lisa decided. It was all mind shattering, and she could scarcely concentrate on what he was saying.

For the next two weeks Lisa ran and played on the beach with Drew, sunbathed, laughed and loved him to distraction. She learned variations of variations that taught her about her own body and her ability to give and express love.

She had been very lighthearted then. Lighthearted and gay.

Lisa climbed out of the shower and forced herself back into the present.

Several hours later she was ready to shoot her first scene with Drew. When she spotted him across the room that had been set up to resemble a ballroom, her heart sank.

He met her look with a cold calmness that was a far cry from her memories of him earlier that morning. Gone was the lighthearted, teasing lover she had been remembering.

"Places, everybody," Tom announced to the group of extras standing around in resplendent finery.

They were filming the night that Reynaldo and Conchita first met. Her father had arranged a ball to celebrate her birthday. Lisa knew she looked very young and chaste in her costume, and she hoped the camera wouldn't pick up the results of her sleepless night.

Richard greeted her with a wink and a smile, placed her hand on his arm and solemnly led her out onto the dance floor while the camera dutifully recorded the pomp of the occasion.

Music filled the area, and as the camera panned the room Richard took the opportunity to say, "What's wrong, Lisa?"

She smiled brilliantly up at him, hoping she was successfully portraying a young, vibrantly happy woman.

"Did you and Drew have words, by chance? He came in to breakfast this morning looking like a thundercloud. It may have been my imagination but I got the strong impression that I was the one he wanted to rain on."

Lisa's smile became more natural at Richard's gentle humor. "He believes you and I are lovers."

"I'm delighted to hear that. I've always said that being shot by a jealous husband is the only way to go." The camera was on them, and Richard became the distinguished father of the guest of honor, his demeanor regal, his face sternly proud.

With her back to the camera, Lisa said, "Drew agreed to the divorce last night."

"I see. And you are both deliriously happy—that's certainly plain to see." He tilted his head slightly to the side. "Tell him the truth, Lisa. He deserves to know."

"Cut! All right, everybody, let's take a twenty-minute break and come back for the scene when Reynaldo asks Conchita to dance." Richard and Lisa stopped dancing and listened to Tom's instructions. Then Lisa turned back to Richard.

"There's no reason to tell him now. He's accepted the idea of a divorce."

"Because of a deliberate deception on your part. You're not being fair to either one of you."

"Life isn't always fair, Richard. I thought we decided that a few days ago."

He shrugged. "All right. But I believe you're making a grave error in judgment." He leaned over and kissed her on her forehead. "That's all the sage advice I intend to hand out." Richard gave her a half wave and walked away.

"Very touching. Was that supposed to be a fatherly kiss just now?"

Lisa spun around. "Hello, Drew, I didn't see you."

"I'm not surprised. You were too wrapped up in what the revered Mr. Driscoll had to say to notice anything around you." Lisa could feel the hostility radiating from him.

"I don't want to fight with you, Drew. This is our first scene together. If we're going to make this movie, we're going to have to keep our private lives and personal feelings out of it." She hoped she looked calmer than she felt. Her heart was racing and she felt almost faint.

He stared at her for a moment in silence, then stalked away without comment. She was one cool customer, all right. Didn't even care that her husband was on the sidelines watching her pick out her newest conquest.

You knew this was going to be difficult, Donovan, before you came down here. What he hadn't faced was that it was going to be close to impossible!

If he could only hate her, feel contempt for her. If he could find someone else. But the problem was that he didn't want anyone else. *You poor, stupid bastard.* Hadn't he learned how to live with rejection in his life by now?

Once again the camera was rolling. The music was slower, the melody more romantic and the lights weren't quite as harsh.

"May I have this dance, Senorita Hernandez?" Drew bowed deeply over Lisa's hand. He felt a slight tremor in her fingers and glanced at her from under his thick brows without raising his head.

Shyly, Lisa let her lashes slowly rise until their gazes met. "But we haven't been introduced, senor," she replied hesitantly.

Drew grinned and Lisa felt an ache somewhere deep inside. He looked too good to be real. He wore the black formal wear of the era, the jacket short at his waist, revealing the lithe line of his hips and legs outlined by the snug pants. The ruffled shirt emphasized his masculinity. "But we *have* met, senorita, although it has been several years since I was last in your home. I am Reynaldo Santiago."

"You are Reynaldo?" Quickly she looked around. "Does my father know you have returned?"

His smile widened. "Undoubtedly he will know before the night is over." He raised his eyebrow slightly. "Shall we dance?"

Slowly, Lisa came to her feet. "I was only ten when you left, Senor Santiago. How did you recognize me?"

Drew took Lisa in his arms and began to waltz with her, the camera faithfully following. "I would have recognized those eyes anywhere. Besides, didn't I promise I would come back to you someday?"

Lisa looked up at him in surprise. "But you were only teasing me when you said that."

"Was I?" he asked quizzically.

"But of course."

"Is that why you no longer call me Reynaldo, as you used to?"

She dropped her lashes, effectively hiding her eyes from him. "I'm glad you have returned, Reynaldo," she said softly.

"Cut!" Tom came striding toward them. "I want to do this scene over." He glanced at both of them and shook his head. "I never thought I'd have to ask you two to put more feeling into it, for God's sake, but, Drew, you're holding Lisa like she's got some contagious disease, and you," he turned to Lisa, "are showing as much excitement at seeing Reynaldo again as you would show choosing fish at a seafood market."

He ran his hand through his hair in distraction. "C'mon, you two, loosen up." He turned to the crew. "Let's get the makeup touched up. And Mike, check those lights over there. We can't have them blinking like that while we're filming. It will look like there's a neon sign just off camera!"

The makeup crew hurried to Drew and Lisa who patiently waited while their

makeup was renewed. Lisa wore an elaborate hairdo that had been sprayed so heavily
that it felt like a metal helmet. A cluster of
curls hung over her shoulder.

When the two assistants left them, Drew
looked down at Lisa, then gently traced one
of her curls with his finger.

"I'm sorry I took my bad mood out on
you earlier. It's ridiculous of me to be playing the jealous husband at this stage." He
gave her a half smile. "Will you forgive
me?"

"There's nothing to forgive, Drew. We're
both under a great deal of tension. We just
show it in different ways."

"I know. You flirt with other men—oops,
sorry. I was just trying to make a joke. I'm
afraid my sense of humor has gone on strike
lately." He glanced around at all the activity
around them. "At least let's try to hang on
to the friendship we've shared these past five
years, okay?" Drew squeezed her hand and
it felt to Lisa as though his words had caused
an unseen hand to squeeze her heart as well.

"I'd like that very much," she replied
softly.

"Okay, places everybody. Let's get it right this time, all right, people?" Tom's voice sounded strained.

He's probably wondering if the whole picture is going to be this difficult, Lisa thought with a slight smile. Not if she could help it.

The second shot went much smoother. Drew was more relaxed and flirtatious, and Lisa responded to his lighter mood.

Hours later Drew and Lisa were walking toward their rooms to change for dinner when Drew said, "If you aren't too tired tonight I was wondering if we could rehearse the scene where Conchita slips out to meet Reynaldo in the orchard. There's a full moon tonight. We could block out the scene and go over our lines at the same time."

Lisa knew very well what scene he referred to. It was the first time Reynaldo kissed Conchita. She wondered how much rehearsing he had in mind. She knew she wouldn't be able to handle her reaction to him on a moonlit night in the privacy of the orchard!

She reluctantly shook her head. "Not to-night, Drew. I'm really beat. Perhaps we could go over that scene in the morning. At least we could run over the lines and skip the action."

"The only action in the scene is the kiss," he pointed out.

"Oh." She could feel the heat in her cheeks.

He shrugged. "It was just an idea." He stopped at her door. "Are you coming to dinner?"

She nodded. There would be no more dinner for two in her room. She couldn't handle that.

"I'll see you later, then." With a nonchalant wave Drew went into the room next to hers.

With a sigh, Lisa let herself into her room. Being friends wasn't going to be as easy as it had first sounded. There were unsuspected pitfalls she would have to constantly be on guard against. But she knew she much preferred a friendly Drew to the cold stranger she'd seen for the first time earlier in the day.

* * *

Lisa was awakened the next morning by the gentle patter of rain tapping against the windowpanes. Glancing sleepily at her clock, she discovered she had another hour before her alarm would go off and she turned over, pulling the covers more closely around her shoulders.

Rain. Drew had always enjoyed the rain. She remembered one time . . .

"Let's go for a walk on the beach," Drew suggested one afternoon soon after they'd arrived home from the studio.

Lisa was changing her clothes and she paused, surprised at the suggestion. "In the rain?"

"Of course. Haven't you ever gone walking in the rain?"

"No. I thought Gene Kelly was the only one who did that sort of thing."

"Try it. You might like it."

He leaned against the doorjamb, his endearing grin making him look like a small boy asking if he could go outside to play.

Lisa found a scruffy pair of jeans and a sweatshirt in one of her drawers. "All right.

I just hope you'll be kind and solicitous to me when I catch cold,'' she warned him.

''It will never happen.'' He walked over and pulled out two hooded windbreakers. ''These have been waterproofed.''

Lisa didn't have the heart to point out that the windbreakers would not keep their legs and feet dry, but she no longer cared. She was content to follow Drew's lead and accept any consequences that might occur.

Once they got outside Lisa realized the rain wasn't heavy, nothing like the Midwest downpours that pounded against every surface. This was a gentle, soothing patter against the hood of her jacket, whispering secrets that couldn't quite be understood.

Drew was right. The world appeared different in the rain. A slight mist rolled off the quiet ocean waves as though they were steaming. ''Well? What do you think?'' Drew asked her after a while.

''You're right. This is nice.''

''Stick with me, kid, and I'll show you all the wonders of the world.''

When they returned home they took the chill off by hopping into the hot tub. The steamy water felt good on her chilled limbs, and with a luxurious sigh, Lisa relaxed.

"Don't go to sleep," Drew admonished. He tugged at her hand until she floated over to him. Then he positioned her on his lap until she was facing him, her thighs tucked around his hips. The intimate position would certainly keep her from falling asleep. Being that close to Drew, she quickly discovered that the hot water had no effect on his aroused condition.

"Drew?" she murmured as he slowly lifted her so that her breasts were at his mouth level.

"Hmm?" Clearly he was not concentrating on the conversation. When he lowered her back to his lap, he was inside her and Lisa moaned....

Suddenly she sat up in bed. How in the world was she going to ever get over the man if she kept thinking about him all the time? Her thoughts seemed to be more undisciplined just as she drifted off to sleep at night and when she first awoke each morning. She felt as though thoughts of Drew hovered just on the edge of her consciousness during the day when she kept busy, but when she became quiet they flowed over her, filling her mind with images of happy times, loving times.

Lisa threw the covers off of her and strode to the bathroom. She hoped that Tom had a busy schedule planned for them that day.

"The rain wasn't planned in my production schedule today," Tom announced over breakfast. However, there are a couple of indoor scenes that we could work on instead. I'd like to do the one where Conchita and her sister are discussing Conchita's love for Reynaldo, and her sister is trying to convince her that marriage with Roberto is imperative." He looked around. "Lisa, you and Pamela go directly to wardrobe after breakfast. We'll try to get that scene finished by noon. Maybe the rain will let up by then."

But it was midafternoon before the filming was completed, and the rain seemed to have worsened, if anything. Lisa returned to her room to change clothes. Drew had not had lunch with the cast, and she caught herself wondering where he was. Shaking her head with disgust, Lisa found one of her more colorful sundresses and decided to go to the lounge and have a drink. Perhaps that would relax her.

The first person she saw when she walked into the lounge was Drew. He wasn't alone. The woman sitting close beside him was slender, beautiful and had a flaming head of hair that seemed to brighten the room with its color.

Nobody has hair that color, Lisa decided waspishly. She started over to a small table by the picture window overlooking the pool.

"Lisa! Come join us." Drew motioned to their table.

Is that the type of person he wants to be the mother of his children? Lisa wondered with asperity. With reluctant steps, Lisa approached the table.

Drew stood up and pulled out a chair across from him. "Sit down, Lisa. How did it go today?"

Lisa glanced at the other woman, who gave her a friendly smile. "It was tedious, but we got through it." She looked from

Drew to his companion, waiting for an introduction.

"Lisa, this is Belinda Montgomery. She's here on vacation from Houston."

Lisa nodded. "Hello."

Belinda glanced at Drew with what to Lisa was an unforgivably intimate smile. "Drew and I were just talking about you, Ms. Renee." She gave Lisa a practiced smile that caused Lisa to wonder how much dear Belinda's father had paid the orthodontist to produce such a masterpiece. "I've seen all your pictures and think you're just wonderful."

Belinda's air of appreciative awe suddenly made Lisa feel she'd aged forty years and was being honored for her multitude of years in the movie industry.

"Thank you," was all Lisa would allow herself to say.

"Would you like a glass of ginger ale?" Drew asked Lisa.

"Yes, please."

Drew gave their order to the hovering waiter, and Lisa noted that the other two were drinking an exotic rum drink. She wondered when Drew had decided to switch from ginger ale!

"How long have you been here, Belinda?" Lisa asked in her most polite voice.

"I just arrived last night."

"Alone?" Of course it wasn't any of her business.

"Oh, no! I'd never have the courage to travel in Mexico alone!" Belinda exclaimed.

Good! Lisa thought.

"My mother and father brought me down with them." She leaned forward slightly in a confidential manner, causing the loose folds of her blouse to gape, no doubt leaving a very scenic view for Drew. "You see, my divorce just became final and my folks didn't want me sitting at home moping, so they decided to bring me down here hoping I might meet some interesting people." She glanced at Drew through lowered lashes. "We had no idea they were making a movie down here. I was never so surprised in my life to see Drew Donovan walk through the lobby today!"

Belinda's ingenuous explanation set Lisa's teeth on edge. Good old Drew—the answer to every sad divorcée's prayer! *What did you expect, Lisa, you ninny? Do you think he's going to allow you to vet all his girlfriends? He thinks you don't want him, so it shouldn't really matter to you who he sees!*

With fresh determination, Lisa said, "You really must get Drew to show you some of the sights around the hacienda. This is really a beautiful place, and I know you'll enjoy it." *There. That was gracious enough, wasn't it?*

She wished she knew why Drew appeared to be so amused. He was enjoying this scene—darned if he wasn't. *I refuse to allow him to get the best of me.*

With an innocent smile, Lisa added, "You really should get him to show you the hacienda hot tub. I know you'll enjoy that too."

Drew picked up his fresh drink and gave her a small salute with it. "Touché."

"Oh, do they have a hot tub here?" Belinda asked with anticipation.

Drew touched the end of her nose with the tip of his finger. "We can always find out, can't we?"

Belinda looked a little confused. "But I thought she said—"

Drew interrupted her. "Did Tom indicate what our schedule is for tomorrow?"

"No. He said he'd announce it at dinner."

"I'll have to run him down then to find out. I'm taking Belinda to dinner tonight."

"Oh, how thoughtful of you. I'm sure she appreciates your kindness."

Belinda beamed. "Oh, he's just been marvelous. I still can't believe my luck."

"Neither can I," Lisa muttered into her drink.

Belinda looked totally bewildered when Drew burst out laughing.

Eight

"Adele, I've been trying to reach you for days," Lisa said agitatedly into the phone. "I've never known you to disappear like that before."

Adele's voice sounded hollow, as though she were talking down a long tube. "I just needed to get away for a while, Lisa, that's all. I didn't have any irons in the fire, so decided I deserved a rest."

Lisa sank down on the side of the bed. "Speaking of irons, you must have done fairly well for yourself on this film, didn't you?''

A note of wariness crept into Adele's voice. "What's that supposed to mean? You know exactly what my commission was on your contract. There aren't any surprises in there.''

"Oh, I'm not talking about me, Adele. I'm just admiring how you got Lauraine Snelling's screenplay sold—by promising that Drew and I would do the film.''

The hollow sound of silence echoed over the line between Cuernavaca, Mexico, and Burbank, California.

"How did you learn I represent Lauraine?'' Adele finally asked.

"Tom was obliging enough to explain the arrangement.''

"Good ol' Tom,'' Adele said with a sigh.

"Yes, good ol' Tom. What would we do without him?'' Lisa asked in a saccharine tone.

"You're probably waiting for an explanation,'' Adele began tentatively.

"Oh, I don't think so. I believe the set-up's rather self-explanatory. You probably made enough on this deal to retire, Adele."

"That isn't the reason I did it."

"Whatever you say."

"I thought you and Drew needed some time together so maybe you could work out your problems."

"How considerate of you to think of us, Adele. I'm touched, I really am. And if throwing us together caused us both unnecessary pain and suffering, well, it just helps to build character, right?"

"You both had the option to refuse. Nobody stood with a gun to your head and forced you to sign the contract."

"No, but you used my feelings for Drew. You knew I'd want to help him out if he were in trouble."

"Yes."

"But he wasn't in any financial trouble, was he, Adele?"

"None that I know of."

"And what did Morey tell Drew to get him to sign?"

"Why don't you ask Drew?"

"Because I want you to tell me."

"I'm not really sure what he said to him."

Lisa could hear the note of regret in Adele's voice, and she hardened herself against forgiving her. What she had done was inexcusable. She had lied. Regardless of her motives, she had lied, and as a result of her lies Lisa had to suffer through the following weeks, see Drew every day, film a torrid romance with him, and all because some meddling busybody had decided she knew what was best for the two of them.

"Adele, when I get back to the States, you and I are going to have to sit down together and have a serious talk. I have enjoyed having you as my agent. You've helped my career, you've helped me personally, and I can't forget that. But no one has the right to play God in another person's life. No one."

"I'm sorry you feel that's what I've done, Lisa. I've seen you suffering for the past year. I've seen your love for Drew eating at you and I had hoped that spending some time together would help the two of you to sort through the past and find a workable future together."

"Not to mention that you helped out another client at the same time."

"That's true. I had seen some of Lauraine's work. I asked her if she thought she could write something for the two of you, and that's what she came up with. I thought she did an excellent job."

"So do I," Lisa admitted. "She's got quite a career ahead of her."

"If you and Drew hadn't taken the parts, I think eventually the movie would have been made anyway. But since it was written especially with the two of you in mind, I hoped you would do it." Adele paused. "Lisa, I want you to know that the money had no consideration in what I did. You are more important to me than the commission I made from representing you or Lauraine. I apologize if I hurt you. That was the last thing I wanted to do."

"It isn't so much me, Adele. You've hurt Drew, and he, of all people, is the innocent one in all this."

"Do you mean you consider yourself guilty of something?" Adele asked in amazement.

"Not in any way I can control, but if you'd only told me what you were doing, I would have explained why it won't work. As it is, Drew has agreed to the divorce, so all your plotting and planning came to nothing."

"You don't intend to even try to work things out with him?" It must have been the long distance line, but Lisa thought she could hear pain in Adele's voice.

"I can't, Adele. Please take my word for it that it's better this way—better for both of us."

"I don't have any choice, do I? How are you going to be able to work with him during the next few weeks?"

"With the greatest difficulty, I assure you. But don't worry, Adele—every time I am faced with it, I'll think of you and your pathetic story about how much Drew needed to make this movie. I'm sure that will make me feel better." She placed the phone back into the cradle very quietly.

Why didn't she feel better now that she'd given Adele the tongue-lashing the interfering woman deserved? Because she knew she'd hurt her and she had accomplished nothing else. The contract still stood, the film was in progress and she still had to face Drew day after day, pretending indifference. And she recognized that Adele had sincerely wanted to help.

Lisa crawled into bed and lay silently staring at the ceiling. Never had she felt quite so alone.

"All right, everybody. This is the scene where Conchita has slipped away to meet Reynaldo in the apple orchard. She's never been so bold before, but she wants him to know that she loves him." Tom stood in the middle of a loose circle of people. "I want the small camera to follow her through the archway and down along the path to the trees."

He motioned to Lisa. "Are you ready?"

Lisa nodded. She hadn't seen Drew since that afternoon she'd seen him with Belinda. Tom said he'd asked for a few days off and luckily they had been able to film around him, but now most of the scenes would be between the two of them. Lisa wondered where he had been, and if he had been with Belinda, but knew she had no right to ask.

She glanced over at Drew. She would never get tired of looking at the man. The black suede pants he wore emphasized the strong, muscular build of his legs and the black riding boots carefully molded his calves. His midnight-black silk shirt was half unbuttoned, the sleeves blousing to a tight cuff. A gold medallion hung around his neck. The evening sun picked up glinting highlights from his tawny hair, and Lisa knew that every one of his fans would see him and wish they were the one in his arms.

"All right, everybody. Roll 'em." Tom's voice echoed in her ears.

Lisa, as Conchita, slowly stepped through the heavy wooden door that led to the archway in back of the hacienda. Moving stealthily through the elaborate garden, she paused once again when she neared the gate, quickly looking around for possible eyes watching her. She'd long since gotten used to pretending she was alone in a scene when the reality was that several crew members were watching, not to mention the director, the cameraman dogging her steps, the wardrobe person anxiously watching that her dress didn't tear on a bush or thorn, and the makeup person standing by.

She slipped through the gate and darted down the path, her slippers making no sound. When she reached the center of the orchard, she stopped, bewildered. Where was Reynaldo?

"Reynaldo?" she whispered. The dying sunlight did not reach beneath the trees. Suddenly he stepped out from behind her, making her whirl in fright.

"You came," he stated quietly.

Suddenly shy, she nodded. "I can't stay long. Maria will be looking for me soon."

"Thank you for agreeing to see me."

"You said you had something to tell me."

"Yes. I wanted to be the one to tell you that I'm leaving the valley."

"But why? This is your home!"

Grimly he answered, "Yes, but your father has seen to it that if I stay, my family will suffer."

"My father! Why would he want to do that?"

"You really are an innocent, *niña*. Your father is no fool. He knows why I've stayed here. He knows I've been seeing you."

"But there's nothing wrong with our friendship. Nothing!"

"Perhaps not in your eyes, but in his? Is it possible you are not enthusiastic about your betrothal?"

Conchita gasped. "You know?"

"It's the talk of the valley. With you and Roberto forming an alliance, the entire valley will belong to you some day. I can understand how that would turn your head."

"But it hasn't, Reynaldo. You know that I love you."

"Your father won't even listen to my request to court you, Conchita. He's made it clear you are to marry Roberto. I can do nothing about it. Now that my family is suffering because of my obsession with you, I realize I must leave."

"Oh, Reynaldo, please don't go. I couldn't bear not to see you again."

Drew glanced down at Lisa. She was adorable in the simple costume. The white gauzy material clung precariously to her shoulders, the cap sleeves looking as though they could be moved with ease. Without volition, Drew reached out and edged the sleeve from her shoulder in a move not used in the rehearsal. She looked up at him, startled. He could see the fluttering of her pulse at the base of her neck, exposed by the scooped neckline of the dress. Her waist looked small enough to be spanned by his hands, and once again he let his instincts take over.

Pulling her closer by grasping her waist, he leaned down and placed a featherlike kiss on her exposed shoulder. He could hear the camera still running in the background, and the lights had been carefully set up to denote moonlight sifting through the trees, but all that was of no consequence to Drew. The fantasies that he'd been living with for months had sprung full-blown in his head now that Lisa was near him once again, gazing up at him almost apprehensively, but with love.

Of course she was acting—that was what she was paid to do. But he shouldn't be taking money for this scene because he was living it and treasuring every second.

He lifted her in his arms so that her mouth was close to his and he kissed her—long, soul-searching, draining kisses, showing her how much he'd missed her, how much he loved her and how desperately sorry he was to have to let her go. Her arms went around his neck, and he could feel her trembling against him. It was good to know she wasn't totally unaffected by him.

Then he remembered his lines.

"I want you, Conchita."

He'd almost said Lisa.

"Will you come away with me?"

He had lowered her back to the ground, but his hand had lingered, stroking up to her shoulder and down across her breast so that it was resting lightly on the rounded contour. He could feel her heart pounding.

He was glad for the script, because he couldn't take another rejection from her. In the script she was supposed to agree to run off. He waited for her to deliver her line.

She stared up at him as if she were hypnotized. Drew decided to save the scene by kissing her once more, because it was obvious to him she'd forgotten her lines. Interesting. Lisa was always letter perfect. That kiss must have shaken her as much as it had him.

When he lowered his head once again, she hastily stepped back.

"Not again. Please. Don't kiss me again."

Ad-libs, each word.

"I'll go with you, Reynaldo."

Ah, she remembered.

"But don't kiss me like that. I can no longer think."

Daring to ad-lib as well, Drew smiled—his devilish smile that caused Lisa and twenty million other women to go weak in the knees whenever they saw it—and continued.

"You don't have to think, my love, just feel."

"Cut!" Tom yelled. He stomped over to where they stood, glaring at them both. "Are we filming the same script as you two? I don't recognize very many of these lines."

Drew laughed. He watched with a certain amount of fascination as the rose color climbed into Lisa's face.

"I'm sorry, Tom," she said. "I froze there for a minute and couldn't remember what I was supposed to say. Do you want to redo the scene?" Lisa deliberately turned her shoulder to Drew.

"No, we'll pick up from there. I just wasn't sure where you two were taking us. Do you need to look at the script again?"

If anything, Lisa's face turned an even brighter hue. "No, Tom. I know what I'm supposed to say." She refused to meet Drew's eyes.

When she turned back around, Drew looked at her with an innocent expression.

He'd learned something very important today, but he wasn't sure how he was going to
use it.

Lisa was still attracted to him. If he could
make her face that fact, there just might be
a chance they could use that to rebuild their
relationship. Whoever it was in her life, he
wasn't around at the moment. And Drew
was. He intended to take advantage of the
situation. He smiled to himself. The next
several weeks could be very interesting.

Lisa looked back over the three weeks
they'd been filming in Mexico, amazed on
the one hand that so much time had flown
by so quickly, and on the other hand, how
slowly the time went when she wasn't with
Drew.

She only saw him on the set. She had no
idea where he disappeared to after the filming was over for the day, but rarely did he
join the group for dinner.

However, the daily filming was creating
such a frustrated longing for him she could
scarcely deal with her emotions. It really
wasn't fair that Drew of all people knew how
to arouse her. He knew the exact spot on her

neck to nibble, to caress, and he was taking full advantage of his knowledge, *on camera*.

Tom was ecstatic with the rushes and teased them about the amount of rehearsing necessary to provide such authentic love scenes. He wasn't far from wrong because Drew was deliberately using everything he'd learned in the years they were married to arouse her. And it was working.

By the end of the day she was ready to leap on him. However, as soon as Tom declared that the shooting was over for the day, Drew would casually stroll away from her and start chatting with someone else, just as though the scene had left him totally unmoved. How did he do it? And how did she cope with her reactions?

Lisa tried cold showers but decided they only made her shiver. They certainly didn't help her with calm, tranquil thoughts of anything but Drew. Then she tried some exercises before bedtime, hoping they would relax her, but her body knew they were not the type of exercises it needed or wanted.

Damn the man.

Meanwhile, Drew was suffering very similar reactions, and the reason he avoided her off the set was that he was afraid of losing control some evening and dragging her off to his room, her room or anywhere else that appeared likely.

He wondered who he was trying to punish—himself or her. Granted he could tell he was getting to her, and why not? They had spent many pleasurable hours learning how to enjoy each other, how to please each other and how to satisfy each other. He wondered when she would give in and admit she wanted them to make love. What if she never gave in? What was he going to do? It didn't bear thinking about.

The day Lisa had most been dreading had come. They would be shooting the most provocative scene in the entire film. Conchita and Reynaldo had managed to escape from her father's trap, and they found themselves in the foothills after days and nights of weary travel.

Reynaldo was trying to get to Mexico City, but they were far from the roads that would lead them there. He didn't want Conchita to know they were lost and that their supply of food was perilously low. In order to survive they would have to return to the valley and risk being seen by her father's men. But the valley also offered assistance from friends. It was a risk they had to take.

When Conchita awakened, Reynaldo had food prepared for her to eat and afterward he suggested she might wish to bathe in the stream nearby.

Although they had been together for almost a week, they had not made love, and the tension between the two was intense. Reynaldo had intended to take her to the priest to marry them, but when their plans to leave together had been prematurely discovered, they had barely managed to get away.

Reynaldo, an honorable man, did not want to take advantage of their situation, but he was young and in love, and hot blood coursed through his veins.

Conchita, on the other hand, was elated to have eluded her father and no longer cared about their situation. Unaware of the dangers and the lack of food, she was content to be with Reynaldo and ready to offer him her love and devotion in whatever form he wished.

Although raised modestly, Conchita was not ashamed of her body nor was she ashamed of the love she felt for Reynaldo, which was why she returned from the river with only a small towel for cover.

Since this scene was being shot in the foothills overlooking the hacienda, Tom had brought only a minimum crew. He was sensitive to the delicate nature of such a scene, and Lisa appreciated his thoughtfulness in providing them with temporary shelter where they were to change their clothes.

Lisa was a great deal more nervous over this scene than the mythical Conchita would have been, she was sure. Conchita had no doubts about what she wanted. Lisa didn't know how she was going to be able to survive any more of Drew's knowledgeable lovemaking. But when she stepped out of her dressing area she noticed that Drew didn't look any happier than she did. Perhaps the strain was getting to him as well.

Drew watched Lisa step from her dressing room in a short toweling robe that left little

to the imagination, and he found himself resenting every male eye that was going to see
her in this film. Not that he had any doubts
that Tom would provide tasteful footage, but
getting ready for the scenes, rehearsing the
scenes, then shooting them would entail
more exposure of Lisa's body than Drew felt
he wanted to share—with Tom, the cameraman or anyone else. He watched her step
hesitantly across the rough ground and perch
on a large boulder.

Tom had already cleared the small grassy
area of rocks and anything sharp that might
gouge one of them at an inopportune moment. A blanket lay spread out, waiting for
them. Drew looked around with disgust.
Dammit. Why did the public insist on more
explicit love scenes? What had happened to
the imagination of the viewers? *Gone with
the Wind* had no nudity, but the love scenes
couldn't have been more sizzling.

He shook his head. *Gone with the Wind*
had been made almost fifty years ago. Suddenly he felt old. He wondered just how
much of his acting ability was admired by
those who flocked to see him and how much

of his popularity was due to his photogenic backside. He realized he probably didn't want to know the answer.

"Ready, Drew?" Tom called.

As ready as I'll ever be, he decided with a grim smile. *I just hope to hell I can remember that other people are around so I don't embarrass both of us.*

The first part of the scene went well. Conchita demurely appeared back in camp with only her towel. She waited for Reynaldo to turn away from the campfire, then she slowly dropped the towel. The camera was given a full view of her beautiful backside but Drew was to react to the view from the front.

It didn't take much acting on his part.

She stood proudly before him, her chin tilted slightly, and waited for him. Drew slowly came toward her, savoring her, loving her, trying to remember that he was Reynaldo, and that he was supposed to fight the reaction he was feeling. He whimsically wondered if Tom would forgive him if he ruined the first scene by tossing Lisa onto the blanket, making mad, passionate love to her, then agreeing to reshoot the scene. Somehow he doubted that either Tom or Lisa would understand.

"Conchita, love, I mustn't touch you."

He paused in front of her, within arm's reach, his body straining toward her, his arms at his sides.

Shy now that she was face-to-face with him, she drew the towel to her breasts, which left the clean line of her shoulders, tiny waist and curving hips clearly defined.

"You don't want me?" she asked.

Reynaldo groaned. "I am on fire for you, *mí corazón*. But the priest has not blessed our union."

She smiled and the camera moved in for a close-up.

Drew stiffened as the cameraman moved in. It was all he could do to keep from grabbing the blanket and shoving it around Lisa's shoulders. *Cool it, Donovan. The man's a professional.* Somehow that didn't help. Drew considered himself a professional as well. In fact he had been part of many scenes similar to this, and his leading lady's lack of clothing had never bothered him before.

But Lisa was different.

"God has blessed or union, Reynaldo. He has brought us here safely. I am yours now."

He stared down at her and saw the glint of humor in her eyes. So she thought this was funny, did she? Gently he picked her up, and carrying her like precious, breakable cargo, he walked over to the blanket, coming down with her so that his body shielded her from the ever-seeing eye of the camera.

Lisa unbuttoned his shirt at the wrists, then down the front, shyly pulling it from his shoulders. While the camera was trained on their faces and shoulders, Drew pulled off his pants so that both of them were nude. In that position the camera would be able to pick up angles of his back, hips and thighs and only see glimpses of her, perhaps a titillating view of a rosy peak, but for the most part the emphasis would be on their expressions and reactions to each other.

Neither one of them had to fake feelings.

For the first time in a year Drew felt Lisa's warm, loving body pressed boldly against his. A shock went through him when he faced the possibility that she could have made this movie with someone else.

But Tom had said it had been written especially for them. The writer knew they were married and had used that knowledge to add sensuality to the scene. There was no way Drew could have allowed another man to hold Lisa like this, to place nibbling little kisses along her forehead and brows, to discover the delicate scent behind her ears, to find solace in the possession of her mouth as it met his with fierce tenderness.

Lisa was his. Somehow he would convince her of that.

Lisa could feel Drew's reaction to their position, and she fought a moment of panic. Never had they been completely nude in a love scene where their reactions could be monitored. She glanced up at him—so close above her—and saw the dancing lights in his eyes. Why had she thought he would be embarrassed by the fact that he was turned on by her? He was amused that she was!

He muttered a few words of love in Spanish, staying faithfully with the script, while his hands leisurely explored the tempting contours of her body. She wondered how much of the scene was on camera and could only hope they wouldn't have to reshoot it. Her blood pressure wouldn't be able to stand it.

When his lips found hers, Lisa found herself relaxing in his arms. This was Drew and it was real. She knew he loved her—and she loved him—and for this little while she could rejoice in their closeness.

Nine

"That's a wrap," Tom shouted exultantly, "and it's going to be a winner. Whew! I think you must have raised everyone's temperature at least ten degrees with that last kiss."

The assembled group broke into laughter, relieved to be through with the scene. The sun had been beating down on them all morning, and everyone was limp with the heat.

Everyone but Drew and Lisa.

Lisa had been handed her robe and Drew his as soon as the scene was completed, and both of them wordlessly returned to their miniscule dressing rooms to dress. By the time they came out, Tom had announced to the crew that they had the rest of the day off. He wanted to get this particular film developed to make sure nothing was wrong with it before they went on. In the meantime, everyone was awarded free time and the group started piling into their Jeeps, reveling in the idea of jumping into the hacienda swimming pool as soon as they returned.

Drew and Lisa were conspicuously quiet in the rowdy group.

Tom congratulated everyone on the teamwork, pointing out they were ahead of their shooting schedule. By the time they returned to the hacienda, everyone was in a holiday mood. Everyone except Drew and Lisa.

Lisa had ridden in a different Jeep from Drew, and she was one of the first to hop out and head for her room. She didn't look around to see where Drew was. She didn't want to know. She just knew that she had to reach some privacy as soon as possible before she fell apart. The quivering inside her that had started at Drew's first touch had never lessened, and she ached with wanting him.

She felt beaten. By the time she reached her room she was almost running, and she stopped only long enough to throw her clothes off before she went into the bathroom and stepped into the shower. A bitterly cold shower. Her head hurt, no doubt because of the sun and the even hotter tension.

Thank God the scene was over. Surely there would be nothing wrong with the film. They had working with them an award-winning cameraman who knew his business.

When she stepped out of the shower, Lisa was numb. Listlessly drying herself, she slowly reentered her room—and found Drew stretched out on the bed, waiting for her.

She wondered when he'd had time to shower, but it was obvious from his damp hair that he had. If it had been a cold shower it hadn't worked for him either, because his naked body proudly proclaimed his aroused condition.

Lisa stood at the end of the bed, staring at him. Now she had the opportunity to appreciate his well-toned body and the way the light golden hair made swirling designs on his abdomen and legs. When her gaze finally met his, she knew she wasn't going to struggle anymore against their love for each other.

She sat down at the edge of the bed, only inches away from him. How many nights had she hungered for him? How many nights had she relived the loving memories? Now she had a chance to reenact some of them.

Slowly she leaned over and kissed him on his thigh, and she felt the shock of her kiss run through him. Then Lisa began to love him with all the experience she'd gained in his bed—which was considerable—and she knew by the groan he uttered that her skills had not been forgotten.

But then he grabbed her, pulling her on top of him so that her luscious, well-rounded breasts rested near his lips, and he began to sip her sweetness, to savor her taste and the

soft scent of her, to revel in the joy of possessing her again.

It had been a long time—for both of
them—and their impatience overcame their
need to savor and enjoy. Drew rolled over,
tucking Lisa beneath him and in one smooth
surge possessed her—completely, joyously,
familiarly and with total love and commitment. She was his. How could she have ever
thought differently?

Drew and Lisa lost track of time that afternoon. They made love, and slept, called
for room service and food, made love again
and slept. But they didn't talk about anything but how to give pleasure to the other.
It was as though both of them refused to
think past the moment, but were determined to enjoy what they had, what each of
them had considered lost, and hoped it
would be enough.

Drew seemed insatiable. His hands con-
tinually stroked and loved her, exploring
each and every part of her, taking enjoy-
ment from her obvious pleasure in what he
was doing to her.

Lisa reciprocated. When Drew seemed too weak to ever move again she would take over, starting at his feet, kissing and nibbling, lightly brushing him with her eyelashes until he was once again reaching for her, his body surging toward her in a need for completion.

They fell into exhausted sleep sometime during the early hours of the morning, wrapped in each other's arms.

The rude jangling of the phone finally roused them. Since it was closest to Drew, he reached for it. Dragging it to his ear, he growled, "Donovan."

Tom laughed. "Ah, so there you are. I'd given up trying to find you and decided to see if Lisa knew where you might be."

"Whaddaya want, Tom," Drew grumbled, still half asleep.

"I'd like to continue with the movie we're making, old buddy. However, you should have been with makeup over an hour ago, which is putting a slight crimp in the shooting schedule."

Drew tried to sit up, but Lisa was still curled contentedly on his right arm and shoulder. "What time is it?"

"Eight o'clock."

"Damn."

"Yes, that did come to mind, although I had several other more useful expressions."

"I'm sorry, Tom. I forgot to set an alarm."

"The question is—how soon can you be ready?"

Drew wondered if his legs would even support him to walk across the room. How the hell was he expected to work today?

"Give me twenty minutes."

"I'll even give you thirty. Try to get something to eat. You'll be out on horseback during most of today's shooting."

Drew dropped the phone back in its cradle and slid his arm out from under Lisa's head. No sense in disturbing her. They would be using her double for most of the shots today, later dubbing in close-ups of her on the horse.

He distantly noted that his knees *were* weak and wondered if he and Lisa had tried

to break some kind of record yesterday—
and last night and this morning. He ran his
hand through his already disheveled hair.

Whatever the cost, it had been worth it.
While he showered Drew faced the fact that
Lisa could not have responded to him the
way she had if she didn't still love him. He
knew her too well. Her love and her loyalty
were too much a part of her. He felt sure that
there was no other man in her life.

And if there were no other man in her life
then Drew was damned well going to stay in
her life—the closer the better. And he'd
found an effective way of convincing her.

Ten minutes later Drew was having breakfast in the coffee shop, doing his best to ignore Tom's pithy comments regarding
Drew's appetite. Drew's mind was still on
Lisa, wondering if the past twenty-four
hours had changed her mind about their relationship.

Lisa slowly drifted upward through the
swirling veils of sleep, her body relaxed, her
mind at ease. She felt reborn, rejuvenated
and very well loved. Her dreams had been
full of fantasies about Drew.

Drew! Lisa sat up, staring around her room with startled awareness. Bright sunlight peered past the gauzy curtains covering the windows, and she glanced at her watch with dismay. It was almost noon. Slowly she lay back down, her thoughts returning to the day before.

Their actions had been inevitable. She felt that she and Drew had merely continued the script especially written for them. Loving someone meant expressing that love. It had been agony for both of them to try to deny what they felt for each other.

But would Drew see her response to him as a negation of all that she had said? Possibly. And with good reason. How could she expect him to understand that she could make love to him with such fervor and abandon and continue to insist on the divorce.

For the first time Lisa faced the fact that she was going to have to tell Drew the truth. She would have to let the decision be his. That way there was a slim possibility he might choose her despite the fact they could not have a family together.

Lisa was tired of fighting both of them.

With that decision came an inner peace she had tried to gain for months. Eager to be with Drew again, she threw the covers back and bounded from bed. Sore muscles protested and she laughed, a carefree, joyous laugh. Sore muscles or not, she couldn't complain about anything this morning.

Drew was hot and tired. They had been working nonstop since nine o'clock that morning, pausing only for a quick sandwich and thirst-quenching water. Most of what they were getting today were action shots, but there were enough close-ups to ensure he was in most of them.

He could blame the searing rays of the sun for the heat, but he had only himself to blame for being tired. He hadn't gotten much sleep the night before. A small smile hovered around his mouth at the thought. He hoped Lisa had fared better than he had.

Reining his horse back to the place where the action would begin, Drew stood up in the stirrups, trying to stretch his cramped muscles. He was supposed to be chased by the hired hands of Conchita's father in this scene, the camera catching the action as they swept by. If they could get this scene out of the way, they could go back to the hacienda. He was more than ready.

Drew noticed Tom talking to someone, and at first he thought it was Lisa's stand-in until he realized whoever was talking to Tom wasn't in costume. It must be Lisa. He could feel the adrenaline shoot through him. What was she doing out there today?

Tom waved a small red flag, his signal that they were ready to shoot, and Drew forced himself to concentrate. He began the long descent down the narrow trail, glancing over his shoulder and forcing his mount to move rapidly. He heard the noise of the horses much closer than he'd anticipated and with another quick glance behind him to locate them, he leaned over his horse and urged it forward.

Drew enjoyed these scenes. He enjoyed a sense of being a part of the adventure, although Tom had suggested they use a double until the group came closer. The hot wind dried the perspiration clinging to him, and Drew felt the exhilaration of the chase.

The camera was trained on him and as he swung past, the camera moved with him.

Lisa hadn't been able to resist coming out to see Drew. She loved to watch him ride. He rode as though he had been raised on horseback. It was as if he and the horse were able to communicate, each knowing what to expect from the other. The sunlight glinted from Drew's tawny hair and Lisa felt the familiar tingle of wanting to run her fingers through that thick mane of his, smoothing it, then mussing it again for the pleasure of smoothing it once more.

"Cut!" Tom yelled, knowing that Drew might not hear him. The extras on horseback slowed down, all laughing and talking, and Tom turned around and grinned at Lisa. "That was just what I was looking for." He stared at the petite star standing beside him, arrested by the glow that emanated from her. Never had she looked more beautiful.

Drew walked up, leading his horse. His face was flushed and his eyes sparkled. "So what do you think, Tom?"

"I'm pleased. Let's call it a day."

Since it was almost five o'clock they were all ready to drop. Drew walked over and got something to drink from an ice chest sitting nearby. "Want one?" he held it up to Lisa, his first acknowledgment that she was there.

She smiled. "Sure."

Tom had joined the camera crew, leaving the two of them alone.

For a moment Drew and Lisa looked at each other, unsure of what to say, afraid to say the wrong thing, afraid to make assumptions.

Drew handed her the canned soda after he opened it. "I love you, Lisa," he murmured huskily.

Her eyes sparkled as she stared up at him. "I love you too, Drew," she admitted.

He seemed to relax some as he studied her, his drink forgotten in his hand. "Did you sleep all right?" he finally asked.

She laughed. "I slept fine. How about you?"

"The little chance I got, I managed, but I'm feeling the lack of sleep now. Guess I'm too old for such goin's-on," he drawled with a slight grin.

"Oh, I don't know. Your age didn't seem to slow you down last night." She glanced at him from under her lashes.

His arm went around her shoulders, and he pulled her close to his side while he took a large swallow of his drink. "Is that a testimonial?"

"If you feel the need of one."

"Not really. You're the only one I've ever wanted to please."

"Well, *cabellero*—" she poked him lightly in the stomach with her finger "—you certainly managed to do that." She glanced around at the activity of the others. "Let's get a ride back to the hacienda."

The wrangler had long since come for Drew's horse and was busy herding the group back toward the stables. Drew kept his arm around Lisa, liking the feel of her against him, needing the closeness. As tired as he was, he could feel his body reacting to her. She had always had that effect on him.

They walked down the hallway in silence, and Drew paused in front of her door.

"Lisa?"

The warmth of his body had kept her aware of him and now he was pulling away from her, leaving her alone. She glanced up at him. "Yes?"

"I don't want to lose any more of our time together down here. Will you let me move in with you?"

How could she say no when that was what she most wanted. But was it fair to either one of them? "I think we need to talk first."

"Dammit, Lisa, that's all we've done and it's gotten us nowhere. Last night proved we can still communicate. Can't we just leave it at that?"

"I wish it were that simple." She could see the strain on his face. He looked so tired. What difference could it possibly make to the ultimate outcome of their relationship? And in the meantime, they could enjoy today. She opened the door to her room. "Do you want to shower here or down the hall?"

He could feel the thumping if his heart in his chest. Was that a yes or a no? It hadn't sounded like a no. He followed her into the room and closed the door. "I'm all for saving water. I'll shower with you...and I'll move my clothes after dinner,'' he added deliberately.

She stretched up on tiptoe and kissed his chin. "You do that," she said, and turned away from him, stripping her clothes from her body.

Drew forgot the heat, his tiredness and his lack of sleep. He methodically disrobed, his gaze never leaving her. She was going to have a hell of a fight on her hands if she tried to get rid of him again.

Dinner that night was relaxed and boisterous. Everyone was enjoying the stay and already lamenting the fact they only had another week on location before the return to the studios for the final indoor shots to be made on the set.

Drew and Lisa were quiet. They were waiting patiently for dinner to be over so that they could disappear once again into their room. Lisa had promised Drew a back rub, something she did very well, and he was looking forward to it.

Already they had fallen into the familiar routine of working together and Lisa recognized the dangers of their easy resumption of past roles. They were so comfortable with each other that it was easy to forget the very real problems. However, she had made up her mind that tonight she would tell Drew the truth. She could no longer carry the burden alone, particularly since they were once again together.

Drew noticed the tension in Lisa but couldn't understand it. They had gotten ready for bed, she had massaged his back and he was surprised that even through that intimate occupation she seemed to become more distant, rather than less. Consequently, he was no more relaxed than he'd been before.

"What's bothering you, Lisa?"

She had wandered to the window and stood looking out over the moonlit landscape, trying to find the necessary words. Neither one of them had spoken for so long that Drew's voice sounded strident in the quiet room.

Lisa slowly turned away from the tranquil night and faced Drew. "I need to tell you why I'm divorcing you, Drew, and I'm having trouble finding the words."

He absently noted that she spoke in the present tense. She was divorcing him—not, she had filed, or had been planning. Had he been living in some sort of fantasy world since yesterday? Was it possible he'd imagined her response to him?

Lisa caught the wary expression on his face. How many times had she hurt him by not facing him with the truth? Why had she thought a confrontation would be tougher than the innuendos, the half-truths, the outright lies that had littered their discussions like crumpled pages from an otherwise neat and tidy book.

No more. With stern resolution Lisa walked over to the only chair in the room and sat down. Still watching her warily, Drew stretched out on the bed, his arms behind his head, propped against the headboard.

"I never told you about the tests the doctors ran after we lost our baby, Drew." She picked up the tasseled end of her robe sash and restlessly flicked it over her crossed knee. "After I got the results of the tests I had some idea of trying to protect you from what I'd discovered, but it isn't going to work." Her large black eyes suddenly flickered up and her gaze met his. "I can't pretend that I left you because I didn't love you or didn't want to be married to you any longer. Our stay down here has convinced me of that."

"What sort of tests, Lisa?" Drew asked quietly.

"To find out why the baby was stillborn. To see if there was anything that could prevent something like that happening again." She shifted uneasily in her chair. "There isn't. I found out that there's something in my genetic makeup that will mean almost certain death to any child I attempt to bear."

Lisa could no longer sit there. She bounded to her feet and strode across the room, to the end of the bed. "What I found out, Drew, was that I can't have children. The doctor said the odds were enormous against having a normal child—one with even a chance at life." She stopped pacing and stood at the end of the bed, staring at him. "I can't give you the family you want, Drew. So I'm divorcing you. There is no reason why you can't have that family with someone else.''

Drew listened carefully to every word that Lisa uttered, amazed at her calmness and dispassion. Had she been rehearsing a part, he would have stopped her and insisted she do it again with more feeling. She had delivered her lines as though she had overrehearsed, and they came out stilted and lifeless. And yet the meaning of her words had gone through him like a deadly stiletto.

Lisa waited for his reaction, any reaction, but he continued to stare at her as though she'd been speaking in a foreign language. She turned away from him, wondering if she were losing her mind. How many times had she tried to picture his reaction? For some reason, she'd expected the words to create an explosion of emotion from him, either of denial or disbelief, or a possible disclaimer of the need for her to leave.

It was as though Lisa were suddenly an onlooker and she saw them frozen in a tableau, each of them waiting for a gesture or a word from the other to break the tension that surrounded them.

Drew slowly pulled his arms down from behind his head and sat up, each movement precise and deliberate. "How long have you known?" he finally asked in a quiet voice.

"Since my six weeks' checkup."

"And you didn't feel that I had the right to the same information? You decided you had the right to make a decision that affects both our lives without allowing me the dignity of taking part in that decision?"

She stood before him, tiny but regal, like a queen before her inquisitioners, her dignity cloaking her like a royal robe. "I was afraid you'd choose to stay with me and later resent the sacrifice."

He stood up. "So instead, you decided we'd both sacrifice—you as a martyr, me like some blind bastard who didn't know what hit him." He stared at her as though he'd never really seen her before. "God, Lisa. I had no idea you could be so deliberately cruel."

"I didn't look at it as being cruel. I considered it a necessity."

"*You* considered it. *You* decided. Who in the hell appointed *you* God, Lisa?"

Lisa was suddenly reminded of her conversation with Adele and her self-righteous speech, and for the first time she realized how Drew must be viewing her actions. She remembered how helpless she had felt to discover Adele's machinations; how angry she was to have such little control over what was happening in her life, and she had an explosive insight into what Drew must be feeling at the moment.

"I'm sorry," she said softly.

He continued to stare at her while twin expressions of distaste and disgust danced across his face. "You're sorry?" he repeated with angry disbelief. "You've gone to great lengths to destroy everything you and I ever shared or hoped to share and all you can say is 'I'm sorry'?" Drew ran his hand through his hair, suddenly feeling trapped in the room.

Grabbing a pair of denims lying nearby, he pulled them on. Then he found a shirt he'd had on earlier. He pulled on his socks and shoes and strode to the door. "I need some air," he muttered, refusing to look at her. He jerked open the door and walked out, slamming it behind him.

Now what? she wondered. *Where do we go from here?* Her actions as viewed through Drew's eyes had been less than admirable and showed a great deal of immaturity. Would he consider the fact that she had still been in shock over their baby's death? But then, so had he, and he still had to live with her walking out on him.

Lisa sank down on the side of the bed. She had always been impulsive, had always been a worrier and had often wondered if perhaps she and Chicken Little had a great deal in common.

Had she unnecessarily destroyed a marriage? She still didn't know how Drew felt about the actual news. He was too incensed over the delay in his learning about it.

Lisa could not find it in her heart to blame him.

Ten

───

Drew found himself in the orchard behind the hacienda, the moonlight creating patterns of light and shadow through the limbs. He walked to the far side of the trees so that the hacienda was hidden from view.

He wanted to be alone. He wanted to think instead of feel. Wearily he ran his hand over his face. God, but he was tired of emotions. They ate at him. They would never leave him alone. His feelings for Lisa felt like a voracious animal, constantly chewing at him whenever he had tried to relax during the months they had been apart.

Drew had tried to view that time as a necessary healing period for both of them. Now he had to face the fact that Lisa had never meant the separation to be temporary. She had arbitrarily decided their future for them and for a little while back there in that room he'd felt such a fierce anger—almost a hatred toward her—that it had frightened him. How could she have ignored every principle of communication needed in a successful marriage—the need to be open, honest and share your feelings, even those negative feelings that appeared at times to be so destructive to a relationship? But she had decided instead to make an unilateral decision, without giving him the opportunity to face the problem, either by himself or with her.

The walk had helped to relieve some of the violent emotions churning within him, and now he had to face the reality of what she had told them.

Lisa would never be the mother of his children.

He still found that knowledge unbelievable. In fact, he refused to believe it until he had an opportunity to talk with the doctor. Had she even considered getting a second opinion? Probably not. Knowing Lisa, he was sure she had heard the news and panicked.

But what if it were true? What if the cold facts remained as Lisa believed them to be. Did he want a family so badly that he would ignore what he and Lisa shared and find someone else?

He shook his head in confusion and dismay. What could she have been thinking of? Didn't she understand anything about him?

Why hadn't she felt comfortable discussing the matter with him? He didn't understand her either. Did she think he saw her as some sort of baby-making machine, to be discarded if it proved defective?

At least he now knew what he was up against. After all those months wondering if she was in love with someone else, picturing her with other men. Some of the images had almost driven him out of his mind.

So she couldn't have children. What was wrong with their adopting children? Had she even considered that? Did she think he wouldn't have a child in his home that wasn't his own flesh and blood? Lisa was one of the few people who knew his background. How could she possibly think he couldn't love any child they took into their home?

He could still feel the anger eating at him, and he forced himself to calm down. He wouldn't be able to forgive her overnight, he knew that. But for both their sakes, he needed to place all his destructive, negative reactions to her news in their proper perspective.

Despite everything, they still loved each other. His feelings concerning love were still pertinent. Love really could work miracles in each of their lives, and maybe God already knew what child or children should be placed in their home to be nurtured by them.

If he could only forgive Lisa her deception.

He thought back over the past few weeks and the circumstances that had brought them together. If Lisa hadn't needed the money so badly, she would never have agreed to do this film with him. If she hadn't done the film, he recognized now, he would probably never have learned the truth.

She hadn't been able to hide her feelings for him once they were together again. Drew found it significant that Lisa had decided to tell him the truth—at long last. He'd been so braced to receive unpleasant news that, at the time, he hadn't paid much attention to how upset she was. How did she feel about their relationship now? Did she want to continue it?

Drew recalled the early years of their marriage when they'd been building their relationship. Now was the time when they were forced to discover whether that relationship had been built on rock or sand.

"Oh, Lisa, if only you'd told me sooner," he muttered. What would he have done or said then that he couldn't do or say now?

Drew spent several hours thinking about his choices.

Lisa glanced at her travel clock beside the bed. Only five minutes had passed since the last time she'd looked. It was almost three o'clock. She knew Drew wouldn't come back to her tonight, and she wondered what he was thinking. Had he gone to his room?

She lay there trying to think of something more she could have said to have made it easier, but nothing came to mind. She had been wrong not to have told him—she knew that now. Twelve months had gone a long way toward easing the pain of losing their baby and then discovering they couldn't have another one.

Why hadn't she trusted him more?

The sound of a key in her door brought her out of a light doze. She watched as the door opened. From the hallway light she saw Drew's silhouette as he quietly came into the room and closed the door behind him. Lisa's heart jerked in her chest so much that she felt sure it was shaking the bed.

Drew walked over to the bed and began undressing. Then he slid into bed beside her.

"Lisa?"

She turned over, facing him. "Yes?"

"I'm sorry for getting so angry with you."

"I understand. You were right. I have really made a mess of things."

He pulled her over to him and held her close. "We're going to work it out. Some way, somehow, we're going to make our marriage work. It's too important to give up on."

They lay there together, wondering where to begin.

"Conchita, my love. We must turn back." A weary Reynaldo held the young woman in his arms.

"No, Reynaldo. We can't. If my father catches you, he will kill you."

"Oh, my love, your life is worth so much more to me than mine. You are ill, *querida*, and we must get you to a doctor. I love you too much to risk your

life any longer." The scene took place in the blazing sunlight atop a barren hillside. Reynaldo and Conchita had done their best to escape, but her father's men were relentlessly pursuing them. The heat and the unfamiliar ruggedness of the life they were living had been too much for Conchita, and she had collapsed. Reynaldo knew they would not make it to Mexico City now. All their hopes and dreams were gone. Now they had to face the consequences.

The scene was one of the last they needed to shoot in Mexico and it had been grueling. Everyone's temper was on edge and numerous retakes had been made, either because of

lines that had been flubbed, or, as in one in-
stance, when the camera inadvertently
picked up the white streak of a jet in the
overhead blue of the sky—something not
exactly in keeping with the 1800s.

The palpable tension between Lisa and
Drew had communicated itself to everyone
on the set. In the two days since Lisa had
told Drew why she'd left him, they had done
no more than make casual conversation over
meals and on the set. He continued to stay
with her, but he had made no more overtures to her and Lisa knew in her heart that
he'd made his decision.

For a short while they had been able to
enjoy the vacationlike atmosphere of the
hacienda and to enjoy each other's presence. However, reality has a way of intrud-
ing on the most idyllic times. Nothing had
really changed between them. The divorce
was still pending and Lisa knew she'd made
the correct decision. Obviously Drew had no
intention of suggesting a change.

In the meantime, they had a movie to
complete. Drew's tenderness as Reynaldo
toward his beloved drove a spike into Lisa's
heart. She'd always known he was an excel-

lent actor. The loving expression in his eyes, unseen by the camera, had caused such a pain within her that she had not had to fake the feeling of sickness that Conchita was supposed to be experiencing.

Tom felt confident that the scene they had just finished was going to be a powerful one. Both Drew and Lisa projected such an aura of love and devotion for each other that he wouldn't be surprised to see it picked up on the film. Whatever had happened to cause the two of them to split, it had nothing to do with their obvious love for each other.

Adele and Morey greeted Lisa and Drew when they walked into the lobby that afternoon.

"What the hell are you two doing down here, of all places?" Drew exclaimed, shaking Morey's hand.

Adele watched Lisa for some sign that she had forgiven her for her deception, but Lisa said nothing.

"We happened to be in the neighborhood," Morey explained, "so thought we'd stop by and say hello."

"*Happened* to be in the neighborhood?" Drew repeated. "We aren't exactly near anywhere you could be visiting."

Morey glanced at Adele and smiled. "Oh, I don't know. Acapulco isn't that far away."

Drew watched Adele as she returned Morey's glance with a smile. "Acapulco. Well. How was it?"

Morey looked at Drew blankly. "How was what?"

"Acapulco," Drew answered patiently.

"Uh, oh, it was great. That is, what we saw of it." He looked at Adele with a hint of apology. "We, uh, well, we decided to get married while we were down here. So to be honest, we haven't done much sightseeing."

"Married!" Lisa stared at the older couple with total disbelief. "You two are married?"

"It isn't exactly unheard of, you know," Morey replied.

Drew started laughing and stepped between the uncomfortable couple. "I think it's great." He draped his arms around their shoulders. "That calls for a celebration drink, don't you think?" he asked Lisa.

She was stunned at the news. Adele getting married after all these years? And to Morey, of all people? She shook her head. Who was it who'd said truth was stranger than fiction?

Lisa hugged Adele. "I'm happy for you, Adele. I really am."

Tears formed in Adele's eyes as she peered down at the smaller woman. "Thank you, Lisa."

They both acknowledged their quarrel wasn't going to destroy the relationship they'd shared for so many years.

Later they gathered around a table in the quietly luxurious lounge while Morey brought them up to date on what had been happening since they'd been in Mexico.

Drew seemed more relaxed than he'd been for several days. He pulled Lisa next to his side on the padded bench seat, a possessive arm around her shoulders. Lisa caught Adele's sparkling glance at Drew's unconscious, yet very telling, body language.

Yet, Adele had been instrumental in getting them back together. Lisa believed in Adele's motives—she had wanted her and

Drew to work things out. How could she fault her for that hope?

"It all started when Adele put me up to giving you that sob story about Lisa needing the money she'd make on this film," Morey explained with a wide grin.

"*What?*" both Drew and Lisa shouted in unison.

Morey looked at Adele in surprise. "I thought you told me Lisa found out you had lied to her?"

Adele stared at her new husband and wondered how a man with so much tact and diplomacy could suddenly forget all his training. Perhaps marriage had unhinged him somewhat. She shook her head.

Turning to the other couple, Adele attempted to soothe their feelings. "Lisa discovered that Drew didn't need the money to make this film. I didn't tell her that Drew was told the same story."

Drew and Lisa turned to each other, Lisa hastily pulling away from him. "You mean you thought I needed the money for this film?"

"Are you telling me that *you* thought that *I* needed the money?" he asked with a mingling of disgust and disbelief.

Then they both turned to the other couple and demanded in unison, "How could you say those things!"

Despite the seriousness of the situation, their reactions had comedy overtones and Morey and Adele couldn't resist the humor. They burst out laughing.

Drew turned to Lisa. "I thought you needed the money."

Incensed, Lisa muttered, "And I thought you agreed to make the movie because you wanted to see me again. I never could quite believe that you could have made any bad investments. You've always been so careful with money."

"Bad investments? Is that what they told you?"

They both turned to the other couple and glared.

Still chuckling, Morey wiped his eyes and picked up his glass for another drink. "Such indignation. My God, you two, who do you think you're kidding? You would never have gone along with the idea if we hadn't cooked up something. And it worked. Tom told me the other night on the phone that *Sands of Sierra* is going to be a real blockbuster of a movie. That you've both turned in some fantastic performances, and from my own observation, it certainly hasn't hurt your relationship any. So what's the problem?''

"I don't like being lied to," Drew said quietly, and Lisa vigorously nodded her head in agreement.

"All right. Fair enough. We owe you an apology for not telling you the truth, the whole truth, and nothing but the truth. But did our ruse work?'' he asked with undisguised curiosity. "Or didn't it?''

Drew and Lisa looked at each other once more and each saw his or her own thoughts mirrored in the other's expression. Yes, it had worked, up to a point. At least now they were communicating on certain levels.

Drew slowly turned back to Morey. "Just don't ever let anything like that happen again. I'd hate to lose you as my agent," he said quietly.

Morey nodded. "You have my word on it."

"That's good enough."

Adele thought it was time to change the subject. "How much longer do you have down here?"

"We should be through by the end of the week," Drew answered.

"Then what are your plans?"

Until that moment Drew hadn't allowed himself to think about what would happen to the two of them once they left Medico, but when he heard Adele's question, he knew exactly what they were going to do.

"Well, your devious machinations accomplished one thing for me—I found out why Lisa left me." Once again he pulled her next to him, his arm clamping her along his side. "Lisa found out that there's a possibility she can't have any more children. . . ."

Lisa stirred. A *possibility*! It was much more than a mere possibility!

"But instead of getting a second opinion, or even coming to me and telling me what she learned, Lisa decided to give me my freedom so that I could find happiness, presumably with another woman who would have my children."

"But that's ridiculous!" Morey exclaimed, then grunted when he received a sharp jab in the ribs from Adele's elbow. "I mean, uh, you two have been so happy together and . . ."

"Yes." Drew nodded. "But Lisa felt she knew what was best for both of us. I just found out all this a few days ago."

Lisa could feel the steady rhythm of Drew's heart from her position next to his side and, from the tension she sensed in him, realized he had not forgiven her. She wondered if he ever would.

"What I hope to do when we get back to L.A. is to consult with at least one other doctor, and if all the findings are the same, then we are going to adopt a family of our own."

"We are?" Lisa lifted her gaze to Drew's.

"You better believe it. You are going to be the mother of my children. You are going to continue to be my wife and if you ever attempt another stunt like that again, you will receive the paddling of your life across that delectable backside of yours."

Since the last part of his statement was uttered rather tenderly in a very low voice in the vicinity of Lisa's ear, she didn't feel as rebellious as she might otherwise have felt at the threat.

Adele leaned forward and touched Lisa's hand. "Why didn't you let anyone know, honey? Why did you feel the need to carry such a burden alone?"

"I think it was because I felt so ashamed. There was something wrong with me so that I couldn't have children. My brothers all have children. My sister isn't married so I don't know if she has a similar problem or not. And I felt I was being punished for something."

"Oh, Lisa, I wish I had understood," Drew murmured. He could relate to that feeling of being unworthy. Why else would his parents have abandoned him as a child?

"It was such a relief to finally tell Drew, to be able to share with him what I've been living with for the past year."

The four people sat in silence for a moment, and Drew knew that for Lisa's sake they needed to change the subject.

"So how did getting Lisa and I to make this movie together bring you two together?"

Morey and Adele exchanged glances. Morey explained.

"When Adele first mentioned her idea to me, I told her I wouldn't waste my time or yours in even asking you to do *Sands of Si-*

erra with Lisa." He smiled at Adele. "Of course what Adele didn't know at the time was that she could wrap me around her finger with very little effort, and when she continued to coax me I decided to make my efforts worthwhile. I made her promise me a weekend in Acapulco if I could convince you to take the part."

Drew just shook his head. Everyone had his price, it seemed.

"Actually, I didn't realize that I was part of the Acapulco package or I wouldn't have been so willing to go along with his suggestion," Adele admitted.

"For some reason I don't get the feeling you're sorry," Lisa pointed out.

"Yes and no. I'm sorry I put you through so much additional anguish, Lisa. That was never my intention. I had no idea what I was asking of you and I certainly learned my lesson about interfering in other people's lives." She shook her head. "Never again."

"However," Morey added, "I did manage to coax her away from her work long enough to get acquainted." He wriggled his eyebrows reminiscent of that famous gesture by Groucho Marx and they all burst out laughing, successfully lightening the atmosphere.

Morey and Adele planned to stay the night and were traveling by car the next day to Mexico City. "I thought we might as well make an authentic honeymoon out of this jaunt," Morey explained.

"Do you intend to combine your agencies as well as your personal lives?" Drew asked later over dinner.

"The only decision we've made about our professional lives is that we don't intend to make a decision. Not yet. We have enough adjusting to do without carrying it into the office as well." Morey took Adele's hand and placed it against his cheek. "I've respected this woman for years...loved her for almost as long, and I'm still not sure that I'm not dreaming the whole thing."

Lisa was amazed at the change in the hard-bitten tough-talking agent. Perhaps Drew was right. Love obviously could perform miracles. She was certainly witnessing one!

Hours later Lisa came out of the bathroom and found Drew waiting for her. "I thought you'd be asleep by now," she said, almost shyly. She had purposely stayed in the tub for a lengthy, restful hour, trying to come to grips with all she had learned that day.

Drew hadn't been expecting her to get the divorce. Once again she had read him wrong. What he'd been doing was trying to overcome his anger and hurt over her deception. But it didn't mean that he loved her any less, or that out of anger and bitterness he intended to end the relationship.

How ironic that she, who had been raised in a warm, loving family environment, with all the advantages of a give-and-take relationship, was learning how to make a relationship work from a man who had never known the warmth and security of family life.

She felt humbled.

"I was afraid to go to sleep," Drew responded, stretching where he lay in the middle of the bed, "for fear you'd drown in there and I'd never know it."

"How did you know I hadn't?"

"Because I kept peeking in to see."

"Why didn't you come in and talk to me?"

"I decided you needed the quiet time. You seemed lost in your thoughts."

"I was." She waited a moment, then said, "Drew?"

"Yes, love."

"Do you really want to adopt a child?"

"Children," he corrected. "Yes, of course. Why wouldn't I?"

"I don't know, really. I guess I thought that having children of your own was what was important to you."

"They would be children of my own. Don't you understand that?"

She dropped her robe on the end of the bed and curled up beside him, her head on his chest. "I didn't. But I think I do now." She raised her head, her gaze resting on him. "I love you so much, Drew. No matter how selfish it makes me, I don't want to give you up."

"You have my permission to be selfish like that anytime."

He pulled her on top of him so that her hair formed a veil around them. "You're wearing too many clothes."

Since moving the sheet back to crawl into bed, Lisa had discovered that Drew wasn't hampered by the same condition.

She sat up where she was, her knees coming down on either side of him while she slowly pulled her nightgown over her head.

"I don't know why you bother putting those things on anyway. You never sleep in them," he pointed out.

"Habit, I suppose."

His hands found her warm breasts and gently caressed them. "Let's form some new habits, then."

"Such as?" She leaned down and kissed the tip of his nose.

"Umm, well..." He seemed distracted by the proximity of her breasts to his mouth. "We could..." He paused to taste, then seemed to lose all interest in the conversation. She wriggled slightly, finding her provocative position convenient to other parts of his anatomy.

Lisa stroked his aroused manhood and he groaned. Shifting once again she found a comfortable position that definitely pleased both of them, and she felt his body shudder as she took him inside her. Drew's arms went around her, and Lisa was suddenly transported to the world of sensation. Her mouth found his, and she could taste the minty flavor that would always remind her of him. She could smell the spicy scent of his after-shave, and she could feel him surrounding her as she in turn surrounded him.

Their lovemaking seemed to be enhanced by the discoveries they had made that day about each other. They had seen each other's weaknesses and vulnerabilities, their fears and perhaps unrealistic expectations from the other's point of view, and they discovered how human, how imperfect, they were. And it no longer mattered.

It was enough that they were together, that they loved each other and that they were willing to make their relationship work, despite the pain and anguish they had each suffered.

All those myriad feelings went into the expression of their love for each other.

And hours later, after having fallen into exhausted slumber, Drew reached for Lisa in his sleep, to hold her close to him once more.

Eleven

———

"Mom!" Seven-year-old Andy came tearing into the kitchen. "Come look what Dad and I made out of the sand." His tawny blond hair fell across his forehead and he gazed up at Lisa with dark, almond-shaped eyes.

Lisa smiled at her son, his dark tan setting his blond hair in bold relief. In a few short years he'd look like the typical California surfer. "Can it wait about another five minutes, Andy? Jennifer and I are making cookies and they're almost ready to come out of the oven."

She glanced over at the chubby three-year-old waiting patiently on the bar stool. Her carrot-colored curls surrounded a cherubic face liberally sprinkled with freckles that Drew insisted were angels' kisses.

Andy took a moment to inhale, then he rolled his eyes. "Boy, those smell great. Can I have some?"

"May you have some?"

"Yes, I may?" he suggested hopefully.

Lisa shook her head with mock disapproval. Then she grinned. "We'll have some cookies and lemonade out on the deck in about fifteen minutes. Can you wait that long?"

"Can I? That means, am I able?" He thought about it for a moment. "Yeah, I guess." Then he remembered his original errand. "Then will you come down and see what we've built?"

"You bet." The oven timer went off and Lisa spun around, grabbed a hot pad and removed the cookies. Jennifer clapped her hands with delight, and Lisa discovered the sound of her child's applause was every bit as heartwarming as the ovation of an audience.

"Mom, is there anything to eat? I'm starved." Fourteen-year-old Timothy stood in the doorway, his cut-offs hanging low on his hips, effectively exposing his lean, sun-darkened body.

"Oh, hi, Tim. I didn't know you were back."

"Yeah, Mike had to go to work, so he dropped me off."

"Did you get his car running?"

"Barely. There's still something wrong with the carburetor."

Lisa tried to appear suitably knowledgeable and hoped he wouldn't ask her if she knew what the carburetor on a car did. She had never lied to her children. But then, she didn't like to appear ignorant either.

"Where's Dad?"

Andy answered. "We've been down on the beach. Wanna see what we've made?" He gazed up at his older brother with hope.

Tim dropped his hand on Andy's shoulder. "Sure thing, sport. What have you two been up to?" The two boys left the room.

Lisa quickly refilled the cookie sheet and once again put it in the oven.

"Mommy?" Jennifer asked.

Lisa went over and picked up her daughter. "Yes, love."

"Are you a movie star?"

Lisa laughed. "What makes you ask that?"

"Cause Molly said you and Daddy are movie stars. Are you?"

"I suppose you could call us that."

"Mommy, what's a movie star?"

"Well, it's a person who makes a living making movies."

"Oh. Do you glow like a star?" she asked with interest.

"Not exactly." *I glow because I'm so happy,* Lisa thought with a smile. "Why don't you ask your daddy to explain it to you?" Lisa asked. Drew had a fount of stories for every occasion. She was sure he'd have one to explain being called a star!

Jennifer scampered out of the room on her way to Drew. Lisa followed her to make sure she made it down the steps to the beach safely. She needn't have worried. As soon as Drew saw Jennifer he went over to the bottom of the stairs and waited for her to carefully negotiate her way down.

He saw Lisa and waved. "I understand we're getting fresh out-of-the-oven, super-duper, Lisa-Jennifer homemade cookies in a few minutes."

"Did Andy say all that? I've never heard him string so many words together before."

Drew grinned. "So I added a little description."

"Good. You can add some more description to the answer I gave Jennifer."

"About what?"

"What exactly is a movie star?"

He laughed. "I'll see what I can do." He scooped Jennifer off the second step from the bottom and placed her on his shoulders, then jogged back to where the boys were admiring a sand sculpture. Lisa could hear Jennifer's giggle being carried faintly on the breeze off the ocean.

Lisa shook her head. Drew had a knack for making everything in life appear to be something special, something magical, and Lisa no longer had any doubts about miracles. They really do happen when you believe in them, and expect them.

* * *

Had it been eight years ago since they'd finished filming *Sands of Sierra*? It didn't seem possible. Tom had been right—the picture had been a blockbuster. She and Drew had been nominated for Academy Awards, and although neither had won, Tom had been named Best Director and the love theme from the movie had won Best Song of the year.

What a year that had been. Lisa would never forget it....

"What do you mean, she's pregnant!" Drew exclaimed. "She can't be!"

Dr. Thompson sat across his spacious desk from Drew and Lisa. They had consulted him as soon as they'd returned from Mexico, explained the tests that had been made and had asked for his opinion. He had run interminable tests, many more than Lisa had been subjected to before, and now Lisa and Drew had returned to hear the results.

Dr. Thompson's opening statement was a bombshell.

"I can understand your concern, Mr. Donovan, but I assure you that your wife is pregnant."

Lisa was also in shock. Although she had taken birth control pills for a time after she'd had her baby, she had realized once she'd left Drew that she didn't need them, and since they made her nauseous anyway, had quit taking them.

During their years of marriage, they had both hoped for children and were not in the habit of using birth control methods. How could she have gotten pregnant so easily?

When she questioned the doctor, he smiled. "Abstinence is a great fertility method, but one that is generally ignored. You did say you had not been living with your husband for several months prior to your recent stay in Mexico, isn't that correct?"

Lisa nodded. She remembered their marathon bout after filming the nude love scene and could feel the heat suffuse her body.

Drew leaned forward. "What are her chances of having a safe delivery?"

"Excellent. However, I'm not going to try to guess what the baby's chances are. I do have a suggestion." He studied the couple before him for several minutes. "I would like to closely monitor this pregnancy and study the stages of development, in hopes of discovering where the trouble begins in the cycle. If the problem is caught soon enough, there are certain treatments that have been developed that might save the fetus. Would you be willing to cooperate with us?''

Lisa still couldn't believe it. She was pregnant. She was going to have a baby. There was a chance, a slight chance, that she was going to give Drew a child. The constricted feelings around her lungs eased somewhat. ''I'd be willing to do anything possible to be able to have this baby.''

''I don't want you to get your hopes up. But there is considerable research being done in this area even though we seldom find a pregnancy in its earliest stages, such as yours, that we can study. We make no guarantees, but rest assured we will do everything we can to help you get through the next few months.''

Lisa was so excited on the way home, she was nearly incoherent, while Drew was unusually silent. Finally she could ignore his silence no longer.

''Drew, what's wrong?''

''I'm worried.''

"About the pregnancy?"

"About you."

"I'm fine. The doctor told us there would be no danger to me, not any more than any pregnancy."

"And how are you going to accept the very real possibility that they won't be able to save this one either?"

"Drew! This doesn't sound like you at all. You're beginning to sound like a chronic worrier."

"I'm beginning to believe it may be contagious. Lisa, I just don't want you going off the deep end again. Let's face what is happening realistically and honestly. Even if we can't have children of our own, let's plan to adopt."

"You mean now?"

"That all depends on how you feel about it. Are you up to it emotionally? Physically?"

She thought about it for a few minutes. "Yes, at least I think so. Are you thinking about adopting a baby?"

"No. I'd like to adopt a child that needs a home. So many parents want a brand-new baby. I would like to provide a family for a child who may not be able to find a home anywhere else.''

Lisa felt the tug at her heart. Of course. ''When can we go?'' she asked quietly, and he recognized that she understood what he was saying.

''It may take several months. I don't really know the procedure,'' he cautioned.

''I think it's a good idea, Drew, I really do. It will keep me from sitting around for the next seven months thinking about all the possibilities.'' She leaned over and kissed him. ''Let's get started on that family.''

When she saw seven-year-old Timothy, she knew right away that he belonged to them. He seemed to know it as well.

Tim's father had been killed before he was born and his mother couldn't cope with the loss. Tim was less than three months old when his mother took her own life. Neighbors who knew the circumstances had given the authorities his background, and he was placed in the orphanage, too young to know what he'd lost.

As the time grew closer, Lisa was more and more thankful that Drew had had the foresight to bring Tim into their lives. Whatever happened, they were a family unit.

When Andrew Donovan II arrived in the world, hale and hearty, Drew and Lisa decided not to take another chance. They had enough love and more to share with children, and there were many children who needed that love.

Once again they had applied for another child, but when Beth Stratton called to say they had a newborn she thought they should see, Drew and Lisa went to San Luis immediately—and met Jennifer for the first time.

Because Timothy was dark, like her, and Andy and Jennifer resembled Drew, few people realized that any of their children were adopted. Lisa knew that each of them had been born in her heart—hers and Drew's—and had only been waiting to be found.

"Would you like some help in here?" Drew walked in, holding Jennifer's tiny hand in his large one.

"You could get the lemonade out, if you'd like." Lisa turned off the oven and whisked the last batch of cookies out.

"They smell delicious." Drew picked up the tiny girl beside him. "Did you help make the cookies, honey?"

"Uh-huh."

"Which ones are yours?"

"Oh, Drew, quit teasing her."

Jennifer pointed to the ones on the plate. "Those ones."

"See, she knows." He pulled Lisa into the circle of his arm and whispered in her ear. "How about a date tonight, babe? Just you and me skinny-dipping in the surf. There's supposed to be a full moon."

She grinned. "We'll have to see how long it takes everybody to go to sleep tonight."

"I've got that all figured out. I plan to slip knockout drops in their milk at supper. Everybody will be asleep no later than eight o'clock, guaranteed."

"Oh, Drew, you are absolutely crazy."

He grinned, kissing her with leisurely pleasure. "I know. Crazy about you."

"He's always saying that," Andy complained from the doorway.

Drew's expression became filled with dignity. "That, son, is because it is true. Truth can never be overstated, or overrated." He glanced back at Lisa and murmured, "Just as deceptions can only hurt."

Lisa had already learned that lesson. Thank God she'd been given a second chance to rectify her mistake. Drew's love for her had been mature enough to recognize and accept her frailties.

She intended to spend the rest of her life showing him and their children how well she'd learned the lesson love offers.

* * * * *